FIERCE PRETTY THINGS

BLUE LIGHT BOOKS

What My Last Man Did by Andrea Lewis
Girl with Death Mask by Jennifer Givhan

FIERCE PRETTY THINGS

STORIES

TOM HOWARD

INDIANA UNIVERSITY PRESS

BLUE LIGHT BOOKS

This book is a publication of

Indiana University Press
Office of Scholarly Publishing
Herman B Wells Library 350
1320 East 10th Street
Bloomington, Indiana 47405 USA

iupress.indiana.edu

Manufactured in the
United States of America

Cataloging information is available
from the Library of Congress.

ISBN 978-0-253-04149-4 (paperback)
ISBN 978-0-253-04151-7 (ebook)

1 2 3 4 5   24 23 22 21 20 19

for Abbe

CONTENTS

ACKNOWLEDGMENTS

Warm thanks to the editors and staff of the journals in which these stories first appeared:

"Bandana" appeared in *Willow Springs,* Issue 74, 2014.

"Hildy" appeared in *Masters Review,* September 2015.

"Temple & Vine" appeared in *Bellingham Review,* Issue 70, 2015.

"Fierce Pretty Things" appeared in *Indiana Review,* Issue 40 (2), 2018.

"Scarecrows" appeared in *Ninth Letter,* Issue 15 (2), 2018.

"Grandfather Vampire" appeared in *Broad River Review,* 2014, and also in *Emrys Journal,* Volume 31, 2014.

"The Magnificents" appeared in *Cincinnati Review,* Issue 12 (1), 2015.

"Xiomara" appeared in *Booth,* Volume 9, 2015.

FIERCE PRETTY THINGS

1

Bandana

Over dinner one night I told my dad about the League of Scorpions, just to break up the deathly silence. I told him how the League was a kind of school club, except instead of doing activities and sports and charitable things, the boys in the club mostly punched kids and wore black bandanas and inspired dread. Told him how the leader of the Scorpions, Tripp Nolan, had a tattoo of a scorpion killing a dragon that was eating a shark. My dad said sounds like they're the top dogs in school and I said yeah, that's the case. He said tell me more about the black bandanas and I admitted they were fierce impressive. He said why aren't you in the League of Scorpions, and I said they only take one new kid each year, and he said sorry, I didn't realize you were so unexceptional and lacking in ambition. That didn't make me feel great, so I said you have to beat someone up just to get an application, and I never even threw a punch before. He said you'd better stop talking now because my love for you is diminishing. Said he was glad my brother Quinn was dead so Quinn didn't have to hear me make that comment about how I'd never thrown a punch before. Quinn killed a dozen Talibans with his bare hands before they strapped an IED to his head and blew him all over Kandahar. My dad said Tripp Nolan could probably kill a dozen Talibans with his bare hands, too, sounded like. He said maybe you should focus less on books and more on being worthy of the League of Scorpions. Then he went to his bedroom and turned out the lights and listened to Vic Damone records, which was the only thing that gave peace to his grieving heart now that Quinn was dead and my mother had run off with the bastard Kit Crawford, our former exterminator.

I went to school thinking about who I could beat up without repercussions, main problem being that I didn't hate anybody too much, other than maybe Gary Compton. Gary Compton was already six feet tall in the seventh grade and had to shave twice a day. He was skinny and colorless and gangly like a skeleton, and he had black eyes that shone like demonic marbles. When Gary slapped you or punched you, which was often, he'd look at you with such hatred that you'd start apologizing because you'd think there's no way anyone could look at someone else with that much venom without a damn good reason. After he punched you, Gary would wait a second and then say, "You're a dumb abortion baby." Which didn't make sense, but it made you feel bad. I wouldn't have minded punching Gary Compton. But Gary was second in command of the League of Scorpions.

I settled on Wesley Bloom. Wesley was small and thoughtful and delicate looking. His mom got her hair caught in the mixer blade while working at the salsa plant in Bridgeport, and after she'd been mixed pretty well Wesley's dad jumped in after her, which most people considered more a suicide than a rescue attempt. After that, Wesley moved in with his grandmother, who was blind and half deranged, and started school at Richfield, where he was unpopular because he wore glasses and had a walleye and everybody said Wesley was a gay prince's name. Despite all that, Wesley didn't seem bitter. He made a point of being nice to the kids who were even weirder and less popular. He gave half his lunch away to the Posner twins, whose lunches were regularly stolen by Gary Compton as punishment for them living in a houseboat and being albinos. Wesley just seemed happy to still be alive and part of the world, maybe because he knew that at any moment he or anyone else could fall into a salsa mixer. He spent most of his lunch hours by himself at a picnic bench in the school courtyard, eating the raisins that were left over from his lunch after the Posner twins received their distribution. He sat and ate and sometimes read a comic book or put his head on the table and watched bugs crawl through the grass around his feet. My point is that he was probably the sweetest and most good-natured kid I knew. He forgave everybody for everything. That's why I decided he was the one I should beat up.

I waited at lunchtime until I saw Tripp and Gary Compton and Teddy Nantz walk into the courtyard, wearing their bandanas. When Wesley walked past me with his raisins and carton of milk, I was nervous but also angry. I hated Wesley's glasses and his walleye and his sad little box of raisins, and the more I looked at him the more I hated him. I hated how defenseless he looked more than anything else. It ended up being pretty easy to sock him in the gut. Raisins flew everywhere and Wesley doubled over and fell to the ground. When I tried to get out of the way, I accidentally stepped on his glasses. I felt sort of bad about that so I jumped off right away, but I landed on his milk carton and sprayed milk all over his face while he clutched his stomach. I looked around and Tripp Nolan gave me the nod. Everybody else just laughed at Wesley, who'd been dumb enough to get punched in the stomach and have his glasses broken.

Wesley rolled onto his back and didn't move. I said just get up now, kind of whispering to him, but he didn't even look at me. That made me angry too. Him just lying there, not even bothering to wipe the milk off his face. My dad would've been furious if he'd seen that. So I kicked him one more time because I was so full of hate.

Next day I opened my locker and there was a note inside: "NICE JOB WITH THE WALEYE. RETORN APPLECATION ASAP." The application asked for my name and social security number and for me to list the top seven most terrible things I'd ever done.

"Well, what are you waiting for," my dad said when I showed him the application. I'd already told him what happened in the courtyard, with the raisins flying everywhere. "Sounds like this Bloom had it coming," he said. "Quinn's ghost is probably somewhat less mortified by you being a blood relation today."

I said thanks but was having misgivings. Wesley hadn't shown up for school and I'd had nightmares all night long. I knew better than to admit this fact. Instead, I made up some things for the application that I thought would impress Tripp Nolan, mostly involving bitterness and ethnic hatred, and I slipped the note into Tripp's locker vent the next morning. Wesley still hadn't come to school. By the end of the day there was a black bandana waiting in my locker.

My dad wanted to celebrate, so he told me to wear the bandana and drove me out to the field behind our old house, which we'd had to sell due to hard times, et cetera, after the divorce. Now the bastard Kit Crawford lived in the house with my mother. My dad shot beer bottles off tree stumps for half an hour until Kit came down from the house and said he was going to call the cops this time for sure, while my mom stood at the top of the hill holding her new baby, the Demon Bastard. I waved but I don't think she saw me. My dad shook his fist at Kit and we got in the car and drove away. Even so, he was in pretty good spirits. He said now that I was a member of the League of Scorpions he could stop referring to me as the one who should've died. I said I appreciated that. He turned on Vic Damone and I tried not to think about the squishy sound Wesley's stomach made when I punched him.

My first week as a Scorpion was quiet. We met afternoons in Tripp's garage and he flipped through girlie magazines and talked about people who deserved grievous punishment. This included the president of the United States and left-handers and the principal at Richfield and the gay couple who owned The Gilded Swan taproom and the blacks and a lot of girls he knew and most people named Todd or Jayson with a Y. I just listened. Sometimes I stared at the bandana and reminded myself how important it was. I imagined Quinn standing there with his arms folded over his chest, his clothes covered in Taliban guts, smiling at me. He said, "Someday you might grow up and kill people with your bare hands too." Then his head blew up again and I flinched, and the others

Fierce Pretty Things

stopped what they were doing to stare at me. I tried to explain about Quinn killing a dozen Talibans and getting blown up over in Kandahar and mentioned seeing him there in front of me from time to time. Gary Compton punched me in the shoulder and called me a weird doofus pussy. Tripp said he liked that I hallucinated, that it gave me character. Gary said whatever. Tripp said maybe Gary could take a few lessons in being a badass from the weird doofus pussy, since the rumor was that Wesley Bloom was out of school because he'd overdosed and tried to commit suicide. Meanwhile, Quinn's head was back together, but he kept reaching around behind him to check for explosives. I closed my eyes and ignored him.

A week went by and I went to see Wesley at his house. His grandmother answered the door and I said I was Wesley's friend and she said that was the dumbest thing she'd ever heard, but she told me he was probably at the dump if I wanted to see him. I asked if she needed some help since she was blind and she said fuck off. So I went out to the dump and found Wesley sitting on an old broken console television, holding a gun to his head.

"What the hell are you doing," I said.

"I'm thinking it's better this way," Wesley said.

"It's ass-stupid," I said.

"I'm tired," he said. "Go away."

That would have been a perfect time for me to apologize for beating him up in front of everybody. Or to say that if he could handle his mom and dad falling into the salsa mixer and having a blind grandmother who talked like a pirate then he should be able to handle something like this. Instead, I felt all this anger well up in me. I said, "You walleyed coward. Nobody cares if you're tired. You want to go out like that? You think people talk about you now, wait till they hear you couldn't handle things and blew your own idiot head off."

Wesley lowered the gun and dropped his head and said yeah, that's probably true, and then he lifted the gun and shot me dead.

My body was still falling when I slipped free of myself. It felt good to be out of it, like shrugging off the snowsuit my mom used to make me wear on snow days. I wasn't angry or worried about anything anymore. I thought maybe I'd go see the world, especially the Eiffel Tower and the Great Wall of China and the Aurora Borealis. I'd always wanted to see the Borealis. I figured I didn't have much time before I was sent to hell for being a hateful son of a bitch and turning Wesley into a child murderer.

Then I looked down, and it was a sad little scene to behold. Broken appliances and scraps of lumber and tile everywhere, the ground littered with candy wrappers and raisin boxes and other trash. And me lying dead with a bloody hole in my chest and a dumb look on my face, with Wesley standing over me with the gun.

He stayed like that for a bit, frozen. Then he stood up straight and put the gun to his head, and I yelled out don't you dare blow your brains out. Because if he blew his brains out then I was responsible.

He looked up and spotted my celestial form with his good eye. "You're gonna haunt me till the end of my days then."

"I'm not gonna haunt you," I said. "I just need to make sure you don't kill yourself. My soul's filthy enough."

Wesley nodded and sighed. "Well, I'm just going to jail then anyway."

"They'll put you in juvenile," I argued.

"I imagine I'll get raped there," he said. Not so much complaining as just reporting a fact. "After a while I'll develop some weird personality disorders I guess. I'll be medicated most of the time so I don't injure myself or others. Then when I get out I'll be a homeless person and eat garbage and live under a bridge."

"You're not going to eat garbage and live under a bridge," I yelled. "Why do you have to expect the worst?" Then I thought about it a bit more. I lowered my voice and said, "Never mind. That is probably what'll happen."

"It's okay," Wesley said. "I'm going to call the police now. Thanks for not letting me kill myself I guess."

But I was already thinking. On the one hand he was a murderer, sure. But on the other hand I'd provoked him. I didn't see how it was going to make things any better for anyone by having Wesley get raped in juvenile and then end up eating garbage and living under a bridge.

"You'll have to bury me," I said at last.

It took some time convincing him that this was the best solution. It also took me threatening to haunt him mercilessly if he didn't follow my instructions. I'm not proud of that. But eventually he gave in. Took most of the afternoon for him to dig the hole. When it was done and he'd covered my body up, I had him push an old refrigerator over to hide the gravesite.

It was getting dark by then. We stood together in front of the refrigerator and Wesley said a couple nice words. He said he was sorry for stealing the lives of all my potential children and grandchildren, which hadn't occurred to me until he said it. I told him it was okay and that they'd probably be monsters anyway.

"Now what," he said.

"Lay low," I said. "People will think I ran away. Eventually they'll forget about me and you can go on with your life and be happy."

"As a murderer," he said.

"It's best if you don't keep saying that," I said. I told him to go home and get some sleep. Things would make sense in the morning, I said.

Once he was gone, I hung out for a while at the dump. Mournful cries rose from the graveyard on the other side of the hill. I walked over and stood behind the fence, listening to the dead. They were a regretful bunch, and there was considerable moaning. The town librarian, who drove into a lake with her three girls a few years back, came over and said I was welcome to join in the moaning if I wanted to, even though I wasn't buried on consecrated ground. I said I appreciated that but I needed to think. I told her I was trying to redeem myself a little so my soul wasn't so rotten. She said that always works out well, then rolled her eyes and walked away wringing her hands.

I went home and snuck into my house and spent the night in my room. But I didn't sleep. My dad was up the whole night pacing, which made me feel guilty. Every now and then he looked in my room and I waved a little, but he didn't see me, and even if he had, I thought seeing me waving like that would've been creepy, so I stopped. I had enough to worry about with Wesley. I needed a plan to salvage his soul, or at least to keep him from getting raped and developing weird personality disorders.

In the morning I found him on his way to school. "Just don't be anxious," I said. "Everything's going to be fine."

"I'm thinking it isn't," he said. "Plus, I feel like it's bad that I can see you. Like it means I'm a lunatic and I'm likely to shoot up the school in the near future."

I said that was the exact wrong way to think. I said we were a team. I'd help him put his life back together and become happy, and he'd help me not have such a filthy soul. First thing, I said, was to deal with the rumors in school that he'd tried to kill himself. I suggested he tell people he was recuperating all week from a rattlesnake bite.

"Or I could just tell the truth," he said quietly. "Maybe people would be compassionate if I just say I'd had enough and didn't know what else to do."

I said as his spirit guardian I had to strongly advise against that.

We argued all the way to school, and right away when we walked inside kids started calling him names. Only instead of Walleye and Salsa Boy they called him Prince Valium and said he wasn't even good at killing himself. Wesley went to his locker and didn't say anything. Then Gary Compton showed up wearing his bandana, overflowing with rage, as per usual. Other kids came over to watch. Gary pinned Wesley against the locker and said only cowards took pills to kill themselves, and he asked why Wesley was so damn weak and pitiful.

Wesley said he didn't know why. He said he missed his mom and dad and couldn't help the way his eye looked. Said he wished the world was different, and that other kids liked him or at least left him alone to find whatever happiness he could find. Said he tried to kill himself because nothing made sense anymore and he couldn't see things getting any better. And then, finally, he asked Gary Compton for mercy.

Nobody said a word. You could tell Gary was thinking, even while he was holding Wesley up against the locker. You could tell he knew this was a moment of some importance. I really wished something good would happen for a change. I tried to emanate powerful waves of kindness toward Gary, hoping he'd see the opportunity here. I thought it could be like one of those movies where the bully realizes how rotten he's been, and it turns out he's only rotten because he's secretly sad and miserable and a welfare kid. Then he and Wesley could become friends and everybody would learn a valuable lesson.

"Scorpions show no mercy," Gary said.

He punched Wesley four times in the gut and Wesley cried out that really he'd been bitten by a rattlesnake and was recuperating all week. The kids all laughed and Gary punched him again and took his glasses and stuffed him in the locker and called him a dumb abortion baby. Everybody cheered, and Gary stalked away full of rage.

When the hallway was clear, I stood next to the locker and asked Wesley how he was doing. He didn't answer. I asked if he hated me and he finally said no, he didn't. But I knew he did. He'd never hated before, but he hated me. And I knew that hate would bloom in his soul.

That night I went home and found Quinn sitting on the floor in my bedroom, fieldstripping his rifle.

"I think I'm making a mess of things," I told him.

"What'd you expect?" he said.

"Thanks," I said. "How's Dad doing?"

"He went up to see Kit Crawford today. Accused him and Mom of kidnapping you, then tried to jump Kit. Got knocked around pretty bad and Kit put a restraining order on him." He finished with the rifle and set it down. His hand started shaking right away. Then he looked up as if he'd just remembered I was in the room. He said, "You want a hug or something?"

"'Preciate it," I said, "but no thanks."

"We could go see the Borealis. Before things get worse."

"Things aren't getting worse," I said. "I'm going to fix this." But he'd already forgotten me and was back at work on his rifle.

Wesley was smiling the next morning when I saw him. A weirdo smile, but still a smile. "I know what to do," he said. He said if he became a member of the League of Scorpions all his problems would go away. No one would lay a finger on him again, including Gary Compton. Tripp Nolan would make sure of that. And he'd have a black bandana to boot.

"This idea," I said, "is an abomination."

"Do you have a better one?"

"You could run away," I said. "You could become a train hobo and travel around the country playing your harmonica." He said he didn't play the harmonica and I said he was making it difficult for me to save his soul. I pointed out that everything terrible had happened as a result of me wanting to join the League of Scorpions. I asked who the hell he was planning to beat up. Someone with even more tragedy in his life? A paraplegic maybe? I said I heard Will Spiner's brother didn't have any bones in his legs. Maybe Wesley could knock over his wheelchair. I said more of the same, pretty furious.

Wesley waited until I was done. Then he said, "I was thinking about Gary Compton."

I said I didn't realize Wesley had a sense of humor. But he said he had a plan, and worst case was that the plan backfired and he'd be killed. I said that was a terrible worst case, and the whole point of talking about a worst case is that it's not supposed to be all that bad.

When Gary arrived at school, he headed straight to Wesley again. Lifted him up, punched him in the gut, and stuffed him in the locker to another round of cheers. But when kids started walking away, Wesley called out to Gary through the locker vent and asked him if he wanted to make five thousand dollars.

I shook my head and groaned.

Gary waited until the hallway was clear and then he opened the locker. He said if this was a game he'd have to do something considerably more horrible to him, as per the Scorpion code of honor. Wesley said it was no game. He told Gary he had some insurance money left over from the salsa tragedy. All Gary had to do, he said, was let Wesley knock him down in the courtyard at lunch. Gary said if Wesley thought he was getting into the League of Scorpions, then he, Wesley, was a moron in addition to being a walleyed orphan. Wesley said no, he didn't expect that. But at least other kids would leave him alone then. Gary said he'd think about it. Said he'd give Wesley a signal if he was going to do it.

After Gary left, I said it was too risky. I was skeptical that Gary would settle for five thousand if he thought there was more insurance money waiting for him.

"Won't matter," Wesley said. "I don't even have five thousand."

Fierce Pretty Things

I said I'd stop haunting him if he reconsidered immediately. He ignored me. Lunchtime came around and he went to the courtyard and handed the Posner twins their sandwich halves and their fruit. He ate his raisins and sat quietly under a tree. When the Scorpions showed up, he got to his feet. Gary looked over at him and nodded, and then he and the other Scorpions walked away to practice their hateful glaring. I said there's still time not to do this. But Wesley walked straight over to Gary and shoved him from behind as hard as he could, which wasn't particularly hard.

Gary didn't fall down. He barely moved. He turned to face Wesley and his marble eyes burned. "I changed my mind," he said, and he punched Wesley in the stomach harder than I ever saw anyone punch anyone. Only, when the punch landed it didn't make the weird squishy sound I expected, and Gary's fist bounced off as if he'd punched a brick wall. He clutched his hand and howled, and fell to the ground. Kids came over to watch as Gary curled up and held his busted hand against his chest and cried like a baby. The hand was already swelling up something awful.

Tripp leaned down and said he completely understood that Gary was in a significant amount of pain, but he was going to have to take Gary's bandana now, no hard feelings. Just that a crying Scorpion was unlikely to inspire dread. Then he handed the bandana to Wesley without a word.

Back at Wesley's locker, when he was putting away the tile he'd stuffed inside his shirt before lunch, I said I was disappointed. I said this was turning into a tragedy and it didn't have to be like that. He said things don't always work out the way we want them to, like, for instance, you don't want your mom and dad to fall into a salsa mixer but it happens anyway. Then he tied the bandana around his head and turned away.

Later, I went to Gary Compton's house to see what he was planning. I thought maybe I could at least give Wesley advance warning. The house was gray and dirty on the outside, and I figured it would be a mess on the inside too. Figured he'd have parents who screamed at each other and called Gary names, like Shit-For-Brains. Probably it was always like that, since he was little. Probably when he came home from kindergarten with a macaroni sculpture, his dad tossed it in the garbage and said thanks for ruining our dinner, Shit-For-Brains. I felt bad about that, but Gary was still a monster. Just because his dad threw away his macaroni sculpture and called him Shit-For-Brains didn't mean he could punch kids and call them abortion babies and cause so much fear and dread.

I stepped inside, and it was even filthier than I expected. Garbage covered the living room floor, but in the middle of the garbage was a young kid I figured was Gary's brother. He was hugging his legs and watching a cartoon with no sound. I heard voices down the hallway so I went to investigate and found Gary in the back bedroom standing next to a hospital bed. One of his hands was bandaged and he was using the other to wash his mom's arms and legs with a sponge. When he was done, he checked the levels on her oxygen tank and her morphine drip. He asked her if she needed anything. She said she needed a new liver. She asked if he was trying to poison her and he said no. She asked what day it was and he told her, and then she asked what year it was and he told her that too. She apologized for asking if he was trying to poison her, and he said that's okay. She asked if it would be okay if she slept the rest of the day, and he said yes. He came out of the room and closed the door behind him, then went to the kitchen and washed a few dishes with his good hand. He microwaved a TV dinner, and while it cooked he cleared a space in the garbage for his brother. He set down the TV dinner and told his brother he had to run some errands, but he'd be back and maybe they'd play Crazy Eights. Then he stepped outside and the rage came back as he stormed toward the Bloom house.

Wesley was at the dump, sitting on the refrigerator that was covering my grave. The gun was on the ground a few feet away.

"You need to run," I said. "Your grandmother will tell him you're here."

"Scorpions don't run," he said, and he adjusted his bandana.

"You're not a Scorpion!" I yelled. "You're a sweet kid. Beneath the murderer, I mean."

"Not anymore," he said.

Gary showed up shortly thereafter. Brimming with rage. Hatred flowed out of him, and for the first time I realized there was nothing I

Fierce Pretty Things

could do. Not for Wesley, not for Gary, not for anyone. All I'd done was make things worse.

"There was never any five thousand dollars, was there?" he said.

Wesley shook his head. "You broke your promise anyway."

"I know," Gary said. "And I'm sorry about that. But at this point I still have to kill you."

"I understand that," Wesley said.

Gary picked up the gun from the ground and pointed it at Wesley's chest. I put my head in my hands and closed my eyes.

The gun went off. When I opened my eyes I expected to see Wesley's ghost. But Wesley was still on top of the refrigerator. He was looking down at Gary's body. The gun had backfired, or else Wesley had jammed it. Either way, most of Gary's face was gone and he wasn't moving.

Gary's ghost rose up and looked around, dazed.

"I'm sorry, but you did deserve that," Wesley explained. "The world is most likely better off without you."

So I had to tell Wesley about Gary's mom and about the sponge baths and the morphine drip and about Gary's little brother sitting at home in a pile of garbage and about Crazy Eights. I said now there was nobody to take care of them.

"That means it's your responsibility," Gary said.

Wesley's face went gray, and he said, "I guess that's true." He turned to me and admitted he was beginning to hate me now.

He dug another hole for Gary's body as rain started to fall. Gary and I tried to be encouraging. Wesley tipped the refrigerator onto its side so it would cover both graves, but the refrigerator got stuck in the mud and wouldn't move. By then it was getting dark and Wesley had to go take care of Gary's mom and play Crazy Eights with his little brother before putting him to bed.

Gary told Wesley he'd check back in from time to time, but for now he just wanted to hang out someplace else and empty all the hatred from his soul.

I went home and curled up on the bed and listened to the thunder while Quinn sat at the foot of the bed and played the harmonica. He wasn't any good, but I didn't mind. Every now and then my dad walked in wearing my bandana, eyes hollow and bruised from the beating he'd taken from Kit Crawford.

In the morning the phone rang. Quinn and I listened in. One of my dad's drinking buddies said he heard the rains had dredged up two bodies at the dump. The gun was nearby, too, he said, hidden under a pile of empty raisin boxes. I closed my eyes and hoped my dad wouldn't remember. But he did.

"Bloom," he said.

He hung up the phone and adjusted the bandana on his head. Then he went to get his gun. Quinn shook his head and said we should really just skip town at this point and see the Borealis.

Instead, we rode in the car with my dad to Wesley's house. "There's still time for this not to end horribly," I said.

"*As* horribly," Quinn said. "And he can't hear you."

He parked the car and I raced inside to tell Wesley to get out of town. I said we'd be train hobos. We'd have comical adventures together and daring escapes and moments of sublime, homely grace. Wesley said that really did sound good, especially the grace part. Then he walked outside and went to face my dad, holding his hands out to his sides.

My dad got out of the car and raised his gun. His hands were shaking. He said I've got you now, you coward. You can't run from me.

Wesley said I know. He said I'm ready.

They met in the middle of the yard. My dad pointed his gun at Wesley's head. Quinn stood next to me and put his hand on my shoulder. Rain was falling and I thought this was it, this would bring about the ruin of everyone I knew.

Wesley closed his eyes and waited for the end.

But his head wasn't blown off. My dad dropped to his knees on the wet grass. The gun fell from his hands and his shoulders trembled. I'd never seen him look so old. Rain soaked into the bandana he'd tied around his bald head. He looked down at the earth and said, Oh, my son, my son, what have I done to you. Wesley stepped forward and said no, I was the one who killed your son and I'm the one deserves to be punished. My dad shook his head. Wesley cried I just want to be good again, the way I used to be. My dad sobbed, Me too, me too.

Fierce Pretty Things

Quinn and I only stood there, still and silent in the rain.

Sirens sounded far off. Wesley said at last that he had to go. Said he'd call the police and turn himself in before the end of the day. My dad sat on the grass and rocked like a child, and the rain fell harder.

Wesley cleaned up Gary's house as best he could. He looked in on Gary's mom and said goodbye, and she said thanks and told him she'd miss his walleye. He sat on the living room floor and Gary's brother leaned his head on Wesley's shoulder, and they watched silent cartoons as the last of the daylight slipped away.

I didn't say goodbye. The two of them looked nice sitting together on the floor and I didn't want to bother them. I walked outside with Quinn and he said you sure you're ready, and I said I guess I was. And then we were gone, and everything fell away below us.

And even though I'd made a mess of things, I ached for what I'd lost.

Quinn knew the way. We went north until we couldn't go farther. Overhead, the night sky shimmered, ghostlike, full of color.

Gary Compton was already there, sitting with his head tilted back so he could stare up at the lights. I was pretty tired by then and ready to sleep. I walked over and sat next to Gary. He looked like he'd been crying a little. I didn't say anything, just watched along with him.

"I never knew," he said, "how beautiful it was."

And I said I know, I know, I know.

2

Hildy

I'm on the pier with Hildy behind the Tilt-a-Whirl and the Himalaya, and all at once I get this feeling like the wind's whipping over my grave. From the end of the pier you can see for miles, and the same few houses on each block are always lit, all day and all night long. It's like a constellation you don't know the name of, you just know it's always there and it always looks the same. Only tonight it doesn't look the same. There are dark patches where there never used to be dark patches, like burned-out stars in the sky.

"Hey," says Hildy. "Woody, hey. Why's your face look like that?"

"I'm just thinking," I tell her.

"You're sure you're not gonna have a fit?"

"I'm thinking," I say again. "Can't I be thinking?"

"Just that you look grim, is all. Sometimes you make that face before."

"I'm okay," I say. I try to get back to my thinking and remembering about the wind whipping over my grave and so on.

"I just don't think that's like a normal face," Hildy says.

"Hmm," I say.

"It's just an alarming level of grimness, is the thing."

"Goddamn," I say, and look over at her at last. "It's okay to be grim sometimes, Hildy."

She says that's the truth, with this kind of world-weary sigh, then puts her sombrero back on. All day she's been wearing that sombrero. Said she found it under the boardwalk. She also has on these gold-glittered sunglasses with a giant eyeball sticker on each lens.

A couple dogs are out prowling the beach in the dark, including the yellow lab Hildy tried to adopt back at the beginning of summer.

She says, "Well, could be that you just got to poop."

"I don't have to poop," I say. "Jesus, Hildy, it's just grimness. Why can't it just be plain old grimness?"

"It can be grimness," she says. "You don't gotta yell. I got these ears."

The lab barely turns his head in our direction as he comes out of the shadows into the glow from the Tilt-a-Whirl and the Himalaya. Hildy takes off the sunglasses and stands up and calls out: "Reggie, over here! We're over here! Reggie! Reggie! Reggie! We're over here! Reggie! We're over here! Reggie! Hey! Reggie! Look over here! Reggie! Hey! Reggie!" The whole time she's standing and waving her arms back and forth like a crazy person. The lab throws a weary look in our direction and moves on down the beach.

She sits down and says, "I think maybe Reggie can't hear too good. Like he's got ear worms maybe. You think he's got ear worms?"

"Hildy," I say, "his name's not Reggie. Just because you call him that doesn't make it his name."

She sits back down on the edge of the pier and puts her arms around her shoulders. "I think it's his name," she says under her breath.

She sets the sombrero down and pushes her hair out of her face, which looks sunburned and dirty and kind of weird in the glow from the Tilt-a-Whirl. She's got leaves in her hair too. There aren't any leaves at the shore anywhere I can think of.

"Where'd you get those glasses anyway," I say. I go through the backpack again to make sure everything's still there. Just habit. Most things we keep at the Snack Shack or the house on Poplar, but some things I like to have with us all the time. Flashlight and batteries, a couple books, emergency meds, and so on. A drawing Hildy did for our mom on Mother's Day that she wanted to keep for some reason. Some pictures of the three of us, pre-Cory.

"Pier Three," she says. "Milk jugs. 'Member?"

"Kinda." Thinking that we're running low on antibiotics. And clonazepam, but I already knew that.

Hildy says, "So yeah, I went back and set 'em up and explained the rules to myself. Then I was like, 'Alright, Hildy, now take your time and whatnot. You can do it. Just concentrate.' And I'm like—"

"You don't gotta tell me the whole story," I say. A heavy godforsaken silence follows. I try to wait it out but I can't. I say, "Jesus, okay, you can tell me."

"You sure?"

"I'm sure," I say.

"Well, so then I was like, 'Dang, I got it, you don't gotta lecture me, we're the same age, right?' And so I went around and picked up the first ball and threw it, but I missed pretty bad. Like I don't even know where that ball is anymore. But I said not to worry, I said, 'You're a natural, kid! You sure you're only eleven? You sure you're not a professional ballplayer?' Friendly at first, but then kind of suspicious. I said, 'You trying to pull a fast one on me, kid?' And I'm like, 'No, sir, I'm eleven.' I said you'd vouch for me because you were there when I was born, even though you were only two and maybe didn't remember me being born, because that'd be so weird? But then I was like, 'Dang, I was just kidding, Hildy, I know you're eleven. You go on.' Which was mighty nice, so I said, 'I appreciate that, sir.' Being extra polite and whatnot, thinking maybe it would get me an extra ball?"

The dogs are gone now, slipped into the dark beyond the pier. When I look back to the south I can't even tell which lights are missing anymore. I'm thinking maybe it's all in my head. Maybe the lights aren't going out just yet after all. Other than Pier One, which went dark right after we got here in May.

"I'm glad you finally knocked them down anyway," I tell her. "Just stop saying *whatnot*."

"Sorry, yeah. 'Cept I didn't exactly knock them down, but the thing is that I felt bad for myself, standing there all sad and crazy looking. And I said, I mean the other one of me said, I could maybe borrow one of the prizes? Just one of the small ones?" She turns the glasses over in her lap. "Guess I can take 'em back. You think I ought to?"

I remind her we should only take what we really need.

Hildy blinks down at the glasses. "Yeah, I know," she says. "Just seemed like I needed 'em."

"Forget it," I say. "Let's go. We need to shut things down."

"I wish we could just keep everything on all the time," she says.

I tell her she always says that. Then I get to my feet. "Come on," I say.

"All right. I've got to poop now anyways."

As we leave I sneak a look back toward Pier One. The wind is picking up and the Ferris wheel's moving on its own, which makes me unhappy. Makes me think of ghosts. Or like one weird ghost, maybe, who rides a broken Ferris wheel over and over and never says anything, never even looks at you. I think maybe that would be the worst kind of ghost. Just because he'd look so sad and lonely and terrifying at the same time. Also I hate Ferris wheels.

* * *

It's hot but Hildy still wants to sleep on the roof back at Poplar. She says she feels weird sleeping inside some stranger's house. It's one of the only houses we found that didn't have any dead people in it. But I know what she means.

The roof's got a telescope. We take turns looking for people. Signs of Life, Hildy says. She always gets distracted and ends up pointing the scope at the moon. "Just in case," she says. So mostly it's my job to look for Signs of Life. I've got a whole system. It takes an hour or so to cover everything, about ten miles up and down the beach, and inland too. Hildy's asleep most nights before I'm even halfway done. But I feel better doing it, like I'm taking care of things.

She crawls into her sleeping bag and lines her animal collection around her feet. A couple she brought from home, but most of the animals are from the boardwalk here. An owl, a teddy bear missing an eyeball, a dolphin wearing a little bowler hat, a sad monkey and a happy monkey, an alligator named Russ—he seemed to just have a name right from the beginning, like she recognized him from way back or something—and a half dozen lemurs with yellow eyes.

"Rose and Thorn," she says.

I tell her I'm not in the mood and point the scope toward the south.

"It's tradition," she says. "You got to. Otherwise it's bad luck."

I tell her she can't just start doing something and say it's all of a sudden a tradition.

"That's what a tradition *is*," she says. "I'll start. Unless you want to. I guess you could start. But you want me to start?"

"Go ahead, fine." Keeping my eye on the hardware store a couple miles down the beach. The windows are busted and I can tell the shelves are empty, but the streetlight outside is still working, so I get a nice clear view. Somebody spray-painted something on the brick wall next to the broken windows, these big jagged letters all running together so it looks like some long crazy word that starts with an *O*. But I can't figure it out. I guess I could ride over there sometime, but I never do. Maybe I like the mystery of it.

"Thorn," she says. "No, Rose. No! Thorn. The second hot dog I ate. The first one was pretty bad, and I was like, 'Hildy, maybe the second one is actually pretty good. Maybe the second hot dog convinced the first hot dog to taste all weird and gray and slimy to throw you off, Hildy. And if you don't eat it, you'll never even know you got tricked. You'll never know there's this batshit hot dog conspiracy—'"

"Hildy!" I taught her that word a couple days ago. Now I'm thinking it was a mistake.

"Sorry, so anyways I ate it. Only it wasn't good. It wasn't *worse*, but it *seemed* worse because I guess I raised my expectations about it? Plus I was thinking about the conspiracy and that was getting me worked up maybe."

The streetlight across from the hardware store is moving around in the wind, throwing weird shadows over the store, making it look like someone's moving around in there. But no one's ever moving around. Not there, not anywhere, not ever.

"Dang," Hildy says. "I should've said Reggie's ear worms."

"What's your Rose?" I say.

"You didn't say your Thorn."

I give her the eye.

"You can't always have the same Thorn," she says. "Although I guess it's a pretty good Thorn, considering. So, yeah. My Rose was macaroni dinner."

"Was just plain old macaroni," I say, rolling my eyes a little. I know she can't see me.

She yawns. "Not so much the dinner," she says. "Just afterward. We were sitting there at the Snack Shack and the clouds were rolling in and you said you always liked storms over the water."

"And?"

"That's it." She rolls over in her sleeping bag so her voice is muffled and quiet. "I just liked you saying that, Woody."

A couple minutes later she's asleep.

* * *

In the morning I sweep up the boardwalk a bit. There's more sand every day, and trash that blows in from the streets around the piers. I can't get rid of it all but I don't like to see it pile up.

Afterward I go down to the beach. Sometimes when it's early and the sun's still hanging low over the water, it's like everything is the same as always. It's quiet and still except for the sea wind, and it's like this is just how the world's supposed to be. Usually it doesn't last long. I'll end up seeing something, and I'll remember things aren't the same as always. But not today.

Past Pier One and the Ferris wheel, I find a Coke bottle washed up on the beach. I wipe the sand and the seaweed off and pry out Hildy's cork. With my little finger I reach inside and slip the note free.

Hi there. It's July or August or something here. I guess by the time you get this it'll be the future, which is so weird right? Like maybe I'm an old lady in a crazy sweater by the time you get this. Except by then I hope we already get to meet in person, due to me learning to sail like I told you. Except so far I'm still a beginner and Woody says any ship I sail would be a death-rat. I don't know what a death-rat is. Also I don't know why I'm wearing a crazy sweater when I'm old. I hope things are good on your island. Say hi to whatever your people's names are and enjoy them sunsets. We had macaroni for dinner and it was delicious, and Reggie's got ear worms. Woody hasn't had any fits either. Bye, Hildy.

After I slide the letter back into the bottle and cork it, I walk to the edge of the water and throw it out to sea as hard as I can.

* * *

Hildy spends a couple hours collecting sea glass on the beach while the gulls scream overhead. Farther down the beach are some vultures too. I watch from the pier and read a book.

The wind feels good. When it comes in off the ocean you can't smell anything else. I look back down and try to find my place on the page, but suddenly the words are all gone.

It always takes me by surprise. I don't know why. Just a funny feeling at first, like I know what's coming, not just the fit but all the little details that come with it. The way the wind feels on the back of my head as I start to sweat. The knotty grain of the boardwalk planks under my hands. The exact color of the sky, some deep blue that's never been in the sky before and probably never will again. And the feeling: like the world's not just going to end, but it's already over. Like it was over a long time ago.

Lots of people coming toward me. Shuffling on dumb legs with blank, dead faces. They're not coming for me. It's not like that. They just walk right past and disappear when they reach the end of the pier, like they're all just marching to hell or something. Or to heaven, I guess, except they don't look like they're on their way to heaven. Sometimes they look at me as they go past, which doesn't make me feel too good.

I wave at my mom when I see her but she doesn't notice. So I lie back down on the planks and look up at the sky. All that blue. And indigo, maybe. I don't even know what indigo is, but maybe this is indigo. People rumble past like a thunderstorm on their way to the sea or to hell or wherever.

Sometime later, Hildy leans over me and her tangled hair falls in my face.

"You doing okay now?"

"You don't gotta yell," I tell her. I sit up and look around. The people and the thunder are gone, but my head's still pounding. "How was it," I say.

Hildy says, "You were going, like," and she lets her tongue hang out and she makes like a zombie noise and her eyes roll back in her head. "So kind of batshit, but just regular batshit I guess?"

"You're still yelling," I say.

"Sorry. You take your clonazepam?" She digs around in the backpack.

"Wasn't that bad," I say. I haven't told her I started rationing the pills. Not supposed to ration the clonazepam, but I don't know when we'll find any more. Most of the pharmacies were emptied out a long time ago. At least we can still find amoxicillin sometimes in people's medicine cabinets.

"You see 'em this time?" she asks, and I nod.

"You see Mom?" she asks.

"I saw her."

"What about him?"

"They're not real, Hildy. They're just hallucinations."

"Yeah, but did you see him?"

I shake my head.

"Good," she says. She wraps her arms around herself and the wind blows her hair in a thousand directions. She looks like a wild animal.

After dinner I let her ride the Himalaya for an hour. The Himalaya just goes around and around forever but it whips you from side to side, too, and then there's a switch to make it run backwards. Hildy never gets tired of it, and she usually ends up so hoarse from screaming that she can barely talk the next morning.

Tonight she doesn't scream so much. She's coughing a little when the ride is done.

I ask her how long she's been coughing like that.

"You know I don't keep track of time," she says.

I give her the old eyebrow.

"I'm fine," she says. She asks me if I've still got a headache.

I shake my head. "Doing okay."

"I'm glad," she says.

"You want to ride again?"

"Maybe not," she says. "I guess I'm a little tired. Maybe we can turn in a little early, Woody."

"Okay," I say.

* * *

Hildy stopped talking when she was nine. Nobody knew why. They took her to a psychologist and then a neurologist, too, but nobody could get her to talk or figure out what was wrong.

"At least it's more peaceful," is what Cory said, over dinner. That made me angry, maybe because I was thinking the same thing and I felt bad, I don't know. Maybe because my mom didn't say anything back to him. She should've said something back to him.

Eventually Hildy talked again, but she wasn't the same. She stayed in the shadows and moved soundlessly around the house, like a ghost. Sometimes she'd sing real quiet-like, but it was all nonsense words. Once I caught her just standing in the backyard in the same spot for an hour. Later I asked her what she was doing out there, and she said she thought she was dead. She said she thought maybe that's what it was like to be dead, that maybe you just watch the night fall and the leaves blow all around and the world moves on without you.

That's around the time I started watching Cory a lot, and praying for terrible things.

I was glad when he got sick. And I wasn't too upset when he died, even though I felt responsible. Then everybody else died too. Even

Fierce Pretty Things

though I tried to take it back. I guess that's what happens when you pray for something terrible like that. Now and then I think I should apologize, when I see all those ghosts shuffling past on their way out to the sea. But I never do.

I think about telling Hildy someday. I know I can't. But I guess I think about it.

*   *   *

No moon or stars tonight. Clouds moving in, but I'm hoping the rain will hold off till the morning.

"Read that last one again," says Hildy.

So I read it again.

> I should have been a pair of ragged claws
> Scuttling across the floors of silent seas.

Hildy shivers beside me. "What's it mean," she whispers.

"You always ask me that," I say. "How come you like it so much?"

"I just like the words," she says. "And that part about the yellow fog that curls around the house and falls asleep. It's batshit weird."

"Supposed to be a love song," I say.

"Well, it's got them mermaids at the end," she says.

"You want me to keep reading or you just want to talk about it forever?"

She buries her head against my shoulder and says she wants me to read.

"Hold the flashlight steady, then. And stop picking your butt."

"Sorry," she says.

*   *   *

The rains come in the morning. We spend the day at the Snack Shack, which has an overhang so we can still be outside without getting wet. Hildy reads her sailing book and writes letters to whoever she writes letters to, and asks me how to spell things.

My head's starting to hurt. I go through the atlas trying to figure out where we'll head once the weather gets cold. Summer's coming to an end. I don't even know the date anymore, and Hildy stopped keeping track months ago. But I can tell the days aren't as long.

At one point I look up and Hildy's at the edge of the overhang, trying to get Reggie to come inside. She's down on her knees, coughing, half in and half out of the rain. The dog's just standing there in the middle of the boardwalk with his tongue hanging out, soaked to the bone.

"He don't look right," she says.

"Doesn't," I say.

The Carolinas, maybe. I don't know anything about the Carolinas. But Emerald Isle sounds nice. Sounds like a place Hildy would like, even if it doesn't have a boardwalk. Maybe it won't have any ghosts either. I measure it out: four hundred miles. At least a month to get there on our bikes, which means we've only got a couple more weeks here. Maybe not even that long. I think about Hildy's cough. Wonder if she'll even be able to make the trip. That makes my headache worse. I take out a sheet of paper and start writing a list of what we'll need to pack.

Macaroni
Toothpaste
Toilet paper
Water
Soups

We need to start eating vegetables. I think maybe Carolina has lots of gardens and orchards, and maybe they weren't all burned down like the ones up this way.

Basket (for apples/oranges) (from own orchard)

I rub my forehead and chew on the pen cap, thinking.

Screwdriver and hammers and assorted nails etc.
Medical supplies
Clonazepam
Amoxi

I start hunting around the Snack Shack. "Hey," I say to Hildy. "You seen the backpack?"

She blinks at me a couple times and then her eyes grow huge. She says, "Oh, damn. Damn, Woody, I think I messed up."

Fierce Pretty Things

"What do you mean?"

She says she took it with her in the morning when she went exploring on her bike, so she'd have something to hold treasures. Only maybe she left it somewhere.

My head feels like it's throbbing now, and I ask her where she went.

"Don't get mad at me," she says.

"Jesus, I'm not mad," I say. "Just *tell* me."

"You're yelling, though." She sees my look and says, "Okay, so I don't exactly remember. I was following Reggie so I wasn't paying absolute attention, and also you know I don't have any kind of sense of direction and whatnot. But I'm pretty sure I set it down on Fern."

"Okay then," I say.

"Or Orchid." Hildy looks up at the ceiling. "Some kind of plant or flower name, I'm thinking. Is a fern a plant or a flower?"

"Goddamn it," I say, "there's like a billion streets with flower names here."

"Well, can't we just replace everything anyways?" she asks.

That sets me off. I don't even know why, but it does. I let her have it. I tell her it's a big deal even if she doesn't think it's a big deal. I say she's not the one who's going to have to replace everything, and she's not the one who has to be responsible for both of us, because she's never responsible for anything. Not for herself, not for me, not even for Reggie because he doesn't want to have anything to do with her. Which is a rotten thing to say. Then, getting more rotten by the second, I yell at her for spending her time writing stupid letters that nobody's ever going to read because everybody's dead, while I'm stuck worrying about everything and trying to figure out how we're going to eat and how we're going to stay alive long enough to make it through the goddamn fucking fuck winter.

I don't have any reason to leave, but I feel like I need a dramatic exit. So I run off. Rain's still coming down and I don't have anywhere to go, so I just storm around like an idiot, getting soaked. I walk to the Ferris wheel even though I hate that damn thing, and I stare up at it and let the rain fall in my eyes. By then I'm not angry anymore. Just stupid and wet.

Hildy's gone when I get back. I find her letters, the ones I yelled at her about, all torn up in the garbage. Her bike's gone too.

For the next half hour I ride through the rain looking for her. I figure she's gone south, toward Fern or Orchid, but I don't know if Hildy even knows where those streets are. She could end up anywhere. I head down Atlantic Avenue and cut over every two blocks to go up and down the side streets before coming back to the main strip. I figure she probably crashed her bike and she's lying in a gutter someplace. Probably with her head cracked open. Probably she's looking up at this stupid gray sky and rain's falling in her face while her head's split open, and she's cursing my name as she dies. I don't even blame her.

Two blocks from Orchid, I find her bike propped against the wall next to the empty hardware store. She's standing under the awning and looking in at the empty shelves.

I pull my bike up and lean it against hers. First time I've actually been in front of the place, even though I've watched it through the telescope every night.

"Why'd people just take everything," she says.

"They could get away with it," I tell her.

"But they just died anyway." She turns and looks at me. "I know you're mad because she gave you that backpack and I lost it. But you don't gotta say those things to me."

"I know," I tell her. "I don't know why I did."

"You were just scared." She walks down the street a little ways so she can look at the graffiti. "What's it mean," she says, touching the wall.

"Kids say it when they're done playing," I say. "To let the other kids know they can come out now. It doesn't mean anything."

She drops her hand but keeps staring at the wall for a long time.

"Oh," she says.

*   *   *

Hi there. I know it's been a while but I wasn't feeling great. It's been raining a lot here. Reggie's dead. I guess his name wasn't Reggie though. He was just a dog. Me and Woody were on the beach yesterday morning and we saw the dogs all fighting over something under the boardwalk, and turns out they were fighting over Reggie. He just went in there to die. Isn't that funny

Fierce Pretty Things

that he'd want to go hide somewhere when he died? I don't know, maybe it's not funny. Anyway, they tore him to bits. I'm trying to think of something good to say about that.

Woody had another fit the day after that. But he's okay I think. He said for me to say hello.

You ever read some poem about being a pair of claws? And you're scuttling over the floors of the silent seas? You should read that.

Yours, Hildy.

* * *

Something wakes me up later. Maybe it's because the clouds have broken and the moon's shining down, full bright. Maybe it's something else. Beside me I hear Hildy's breath rattling in her chest.

Standing at the edge of the roof, I look out toward the sea. And something catches the corner of my eye.

Takes me a while to get the telescope set up because I don't want to wake Hildy by turning on the flashlight. At first I don't even know what I'm seeing. Just a flash of reddish-orange light bobbing up and down on the shoreline.

Then I see somebody walking along the beach holding a torch.

My heart's racing. I never thought I'd see anything else alive through that telescope. No matter what I ever said to Hildy.

Once my eyes adjust I see that he's a kid, no older than me. He's just dancing along the beach with this crazy torch, skipping back and forth like he's leading a parade in the middle of the night. In the gloom behind him I can see some others too.

"Hildy," I call out, but she doesn't wake up. I'm about to yell her name when my eyes adjust and I get a better look at who's coming our way.

Two men with long beards trail right behind the boy, and then a little farther back there's a line of women and a couple of kids, moving single file. I can't figure out why they're walking single file like that, and then I see the moonlight glint off the chains between their feet as they shuffle along the sand. Something small, Hildy-sized, is dragging along the sand at the very back, still chained to the others.

I watch them till they're past.

"What is it," says Hildy a couple minutes later, when I lay down next to her.

"Go back to sleep," I say.

* * *

Couple mornings later, I wake up and Hildy's gone.

I go out to the boardwalk and sweep up like always, and then I go down to the beach. I find her hunched over at the end of the pier. Next to her, the sand's splattered with blood.

"Sorry," she says. "Thought I'd feel better by now."

At least I know why we're almost out of amoxicillin. I tell Hildy to get some sleep and then I head out to look for more.

Since we'd come to the beach we always avoided the houses with the red X on the door. But I know where they all are. First two houses I check are locked and the windows are barred. But the back door of the third house is unlocked. Some foul smell breathes out, like I expect. I try to go through the rooms quickly, figuring there can't be anything too good in here. Even if the rooms are empty and I find some antibiotics, there can't be anything good in a house with an X on the door.

The door to the last room on the top floor is pulled shut. For a second I think about leaving and going on to the next house, which maybe doesn't have something awful waiting for me. Because I think that most likely there's a clown in there. A dead clown, holding some rotting flowers or something. I don't know why I think that.

There's no clown, though. Just three bodies on the bed that aren't exactly skeletons, but they don't look like regular dead bodies either. Two little bodies and a bigger, longer body, a mom or a dad, beside them. All wrapped up together on the bed, like they died that way. Or like the two little ones were put there at the end, once it was over, and then the mom or the dad just lay down next to them to die. Which I figure is pretty horrible, but maybe there are more horrible things than to die like that, with your family next to you.

I wish I could do something for them. Somebody ought to do something for everyone when they die. But all I do is go through the medicine cabinet and steal things.

Later I wake Hildy up and hand her some pills.

"Hey," she says. "You can eat me if you got to."

"What the hell," I say.

"I mean if I'm dead and you don't have any choice. I don't mind if you eat me. I won't haunt you or anything, Woody."

I hand her a cup of water. "Thanks," I tell her.

* * *

Some days I think she's doing better.

She doesn't write letters anymore, or at least I don't find bottles on the beach when I go out in the morning. I've taken to writing letters myself, just because I don't want whoever it is to get worried. I don't have a lot to say. Mostly I just say that Hildy's feeling better and we'll see them soon. Once I wrote about seeing that word on the wall, *Ollyollyoxenfree*, and what it meant. Hildy would have told them about that.

* * *

We're out on the beach in the dark, and the ocean is restless and strange. Hildy sits next to me and puts her head on my shoulder.

"I'm glad to be here, Woody," she says.

I tell her I'm glad too.

"I just mean I'm glad I got to be with you."

"You shouldn't talk like that," I tell her.

"I know," she says. "But I'm glad."

We just sit there for a while, listening to the sea. I like having her head on my shoulder, I guess.

* * *

It's a strange thing. Usually I know pretty soon when it's coming on. But this is different. Maybe it's a fit, or maybe it's something else.

I'm with Hildy on the beach. We're pushing a sailboat into the water as the sun sets behind the mainland in the west.

Jump on, I tell her.

I'm trying, I'm trying, she says.

Like I said, it's a strange thing. Because I can see them, Hildy and me, and I can hear them. But I'm back on the shore. I can't say anything. I can only watch them set off, and hear them speak, until they've sailed too far for me to hear them clearly. Then all I hear are a few words here and there, whatever the wind carries ashore. Eventually the words run together and I can't make out who's talking, or what the words even mean.

 . . . *was cold, I remember . . .*
 . . . *ran off and made her so mad . . .*
 . . . *said the mainsail, right there, goddamn it . . .*
 . . . *that dumb song but I still think about it. . .*
 . . . *hard alee, now . . .*
 . . . *like in a million years when it's just fish . . .*
 . . . *even read that sailing book anyway . . .*
 . . . *course I remember . . .*
 . . . *would hold my breath but in a good way . . .*
 . . . *and pipe tobacco and something else . . .*
 . . . *imagined everything, Woody . . .*
 . . . *said starboard, damn . . .*
 . . . *and I was glad, too, even though . . .*
 . . . *I know, Hildy . . .*
 . . . *like indigo and blue and something else . . .*
 . . . *and the whole time we were . . .*
 . . . *yes . . .*
 . . . *just one more . . .*
 . . . *just the beginning, pages are getting wet . . .*
 . . . *I know, I know . . .*
 . . . *let us go, then, you and I . . .*
 . . . *yes, yes, Woody, yes . . .*

And then the words are gone.

Behind me the lights are going out. I'm still here, though. Just waiting. Keeping my eye on things. Until the lights go dark and the sand settles over all of it, over every last inch. I'll be waiting right here on the shore. Just in case they ever come back home.

3

Temple & Vine

Cameron's doing the weird eye-rolling thing when Ruby snaps him into the car seat, never the best sign. She takes the notebook from her purse and scribbles *weird eye-rolling thing, Sat. morning, on way to Bon Soir.* Then she slides the notebook back into her purse and backs the Ghost out of the driveway.

The Ghost is Bill's nickname for the Chevy, which he picked up last year at Mason's Auto Paradise for two hundred dollars on account of it having been the scene of a double murder. "Double murder or murder-suicide?" Bill had asked, but Mason assured him it was just double murder so Bill bought it. It's a good car when it isn't making odd noises, including the horrible wet sighs it makes just before it breaks down.

"Glub-glub," says Cam.

"No glub-glub," Ruby says. "Let's hope not."

"May-bee," he sings. And then, hopefully, "Booger-man?"

Ruby says, "We'll see." She's given up explaining that Burger Man is gone, that he's dancing on some other corner now. Cam doesn't know the other corner is across from Vine Street Park, and she has no urgent need to tell him this, given his recent interest in street maps. He still puzzles over the names, but he knows the little green blobs are parks. Someday soon he'll put his finger down on the green blob that is Vine Street Park and notice it's pretty close to the house and ask why he's been to every other park within ten miles except for that one. As if Ruby has been intentionally avoiding it for his entire life, ha ha.

"We're going to pick up the curtains," she says. "Remember?"

"Gold," he says, drawing the word out with oddball delight. He says "Gold" again, and then again and again, louder each time, until finally it gets weird and Ruby turns up the radio to block it out.

But yes, gold. And thin, and delicate. With a kind of flower pattern thing that she can never remember the name of. Bill would know, something French. The flower pattern thing is so subtle you don't even notice at first. You—if you're someone who notices curtains, for example, Bill's mom, Candice—you might think nice curtains, what with the gold. And well now, you got this kind of flower pattern thing happening, don't you?

She rolls onto Calvert and climbs a corkscrew turn that makes Cam giggle. Not the most direct way to Chez Bon Soir, but it's still five minutes till the shop opens and she likes to build a healthy surplus of goodwill before taking Cam out in public. She'll still be able to run in and pick the curtains up right as they open, then be home with plenty of time to hang them before Bill wakes up.

Sweet Bill. Pulled the blanket over his head last night when he got home and wouldn't speak, even though she knew he was lying there awake forever. Had one of his black days yesterday so she didn't see him much. Spent a lot of time locked in the shed yesterday. But today will be different. He'll wake up and wander into the living room and see all this gold light streaming in through the curtains. And he'll turn to Ruby and shake his head and give her that weird look that she loves, kind of a surprised flinch, or maybe it's some kind of brain damage, but whatever it is, she loves it because she thinks it means he's happy. Not just happy but kind of aware of the goodness of the universe? Which makes *her* aware of the goodness of the universe. She hopes that's what will happen. Hopes he'll give her that flinch, and then maybe he won't say anything for an hour but it'll be the good kind of not-saying-anything, not the I'm-gonna-go-out-and-spend-six-hours-locked-in-the-shed kind of not-saying-anything.

Nine thirty-two. She parks the car and unsnaps Cam from the seat. "Fifteen minutes," she reminds him. "Easy."

"May-bee," he says again. Sounds doubtful. Eyes do a little pre-roll.

The shop is empty except for a tall, pretty blond taking photos of some vintage furniture with her cell phone. Cam finds a Lego roller coaster set on the floor in the corner and crab-walks over to inspect it. Another thing for the notebook. Ruby waits at the counter with her hand hovering over the bell.

Last time she was in the shop hadn't been great. She'd asked about the curtains and Genevieve, the owner, told her the price was two hundred fifty, and Ruby tried hard not to have any visible reaction, except she realized right away that she wasn't blinking, which wasn't normal, but by then she'd gone too far and had to commit to it. Finally with watery eyes she asked about layaway, and the word kind of dropped between her and Genevieve and landed on the counter with a gross thud. "I'm sad and horrible," it cried, and Cam picked that moment to announce that he'd just pooped a lot, "an awful lot," and was in fact still pooping. Genevieve said, "We do have a store credit card if you're unable to pay the full amount now." Ruby concentrated on becoming invisible, really nailing it too, so that Genevieve was able to look right through her and start chatting with another customer. Ruby was left holding an application for a store credit card called VIVA!, which she pretended to read as she floated ghostlike to the door, anchored to the floor only by Cam and his potent smell.

That was two months ago. There's room on the credit card now, and Cam is preoccupied with the coaster. Even so, her stomach clenches when Genevieve appears.

"You came in looking at the curtains, right?" Genevieve smiles brilliantly and nods toward the Lego corner. "I remember the little guy. Pooper." She flashes another hundred-watt smile.

"Yes," says Ruby, off-balance. "Yes, the curtains, I mean. And yeah, he's a handful." She grins and rolls her eyes.

"Think you asked about layaway." Genevieve leans in as if they're sorority sisters, or at least the way Ruby imagines sorority sisters might lean in to each other. She says, "Not our regular policy? But I can probably make it work, sweetheart."

Ruby flinches. Just barely, but it's definitely a flinch, the first she can ever remember. She wonders if this is like Bill's flinch, if it comes from the same place.

"I'm okay," she says, "I mean I have the money, it's okay."

"They're pretty curtains," says Genevieve. Ruby blushes, and then when Genevieve goes to find the curtains Ruby is overcome by a weird dumb gratitude. Not for Genevieve really, but just for the universe slipping this moment in, giving her this.

She's too negative, that's the thing. Always misreading people and thinking the worst. What does she know about Genevieve, anyway? Maybe she was having a bad day last time Ruby came in, or maybe she just has that kind of face that looks bitter and disapproving and she can't help it. She probably looks at puppies and babies with that same face and doesn't get why they cry and shrink away in horror, and it makes her miserable. Which makes her, Genevieve that is, think the world is a sad place that doesn't make any sense at all, and then here comes Ruby to prove her right by clenching up when she walks over, expecting the worst, and all because Genevieve was born with this face that can't do normal face things.

Genevieve finishes ringing up the sale, and she and Ruby are discussing some finer points of decorating when the tall blond screams from the direction of the Lego corner.

Ruby finds Cam knocking his head against the wall, mouth stuffed with Lego pieces. There's a shallow dent in the wall and maybe a smear of blood. No, definitely a smear of blood. Ruby scoops him into her arms and he spits out the Lego pieces and yells that he wants to see Booger-man *now*.

"He shouldn't be unsupervised," the tall blond says, and takes a photo of the dent and the blood smear. And Genevieve says, "I've got bandages in the back," with some real concern but also some doubt, clearly some doubt.

"It's okay," says Ruby. "I mean, I've got tons of bandages in the car." And this is true, but horrible, because who has tons of bandages in her car? Terrible moms do. Moms who need tons of bandages for their bloody, poop-filled kids.

"He's *troubled*," the tall blond declares. "That's *clear*." Click.

"Thank you," Ruby calls out, not wanting to look like she's racing for the door, but well, she's racing for the door.

Cam digs his fingers into the flesh of Ruby's arms, and he leans in close so he can scream directly into her ear as they reach the exit: BOOGER-MAN BOOGER-MAN BOOGER-MAN BOOGER-MAN BOOGER-MAN! Ruby pushes open the door with her foot and Cam kicks her in the kneecap, and she screams back at him: "Okay-okay-okay-okay!" He kicks her kneecap again and goddamn that one really hurt and she yells, "Fucking fuck FUCK!"

The door swings shut behind them. Cam freezes in her arms. Ruby knows without turning around that Genevieve and the tall blond are staring at her. In horror, she has to assume.

After a few seconds Cam touches Ruby's face. He says, voice solemn, "Booger-man?"

"Okay, sure, yeah," she says. "Okay, hell."

She snaps him into the seat and cleans his head and inspects the damage. He's done worse to himself. She knows he'll do worse to himself in the future. For a few seconds this thought just sits there in the front of her mind, quietly expanding to fill the whole space.

Then it fades away, same as always.

She takes out the notebook and scribbles *head-banging thing, plus ate some Legos*. She starts the Ghost and speeds out of the parking lot. A few minutes later she turns onto Vine.

*   *   *

Dale is stuck behind a gold Toyota going fifteen miles an hour. There's time, he thinks. Still plenty of time to get to work. He's only two miles away. No reason to—okay, twelve. Twelve miles an hour. Because that's normal, to slow down like that on an empty road on a Saturday morning. Nothing strange about that. Not as if the driver is some malevolent force bent on making Dale late for work, ha ha! Just a totally normal person who has nothing against Dale, doesn't know that Angel explained just this week that the next time Dale is late for work will be the last time.

"You are already fired," is what Angel actually said. "It is destiny, yes? We will let the rope play out, but you are already fired. I tell you this so that next time we skip this part. I will look at my watch like this, and I will shake my head like this, very sadly. And you will take off the Divine Hamburger costume, and you will leave forever. It's better like this, yes? To have it out of the way."

Coop is curled up in the passenger seat, moaning and holding his stomach, his face pressed against the window. "If you could just maybe pull over," he says. "I'll throw up, then we're good to go."

"Eight!" Dale yells. Eight miles an hour.

They're on Fillmore just south of Third Street, and coming up is a long light, a light that someone should really write to the township about. But they're going to make it, they're close enough now, Dale and the gold Toyota, that they can't possibly miss the light. Unless, oh Jesus, oh sweet Jesus Christ. The light turns yellow and the Toyota's brake lights flash, twenty feet from the intersection.

"Thinking it was a bad taco," says Coop.

Dale closes his eyes.

"Pesticides, then. They're all over everything."

It's occurred to Dale that his brother Cooper's stomach problems are all in his head, since his brother's stomach isn't even technically a thing anymore. But then neither is his head. Coop drank a half-quart of antifreeze when he was seventeen and Dale was ten, dying the same way their father died a couple years before. Even at ten, Dale wondered why they kept storing antifreeze in the garage. Now and then after Coop died he considered throwing it out. It worried him sometimes that he never did.

He punches Angel's number. No answer. He imagines Angel staring at the phone and shaking his head at Dale's number, very sadly. He leaves a message: "So hi Angel, it's me. Dropped Teddy off with his mom this morning and, uh, there's a big wreck, horse trailer, and there's horse parts everywhere, all over the west side, *fuck*." Delete. "Angel, it's me, it's Dale. Be there soon, practically on time I'm thinking, just got stuck at this train crossing? Again? So anyways, *shit*." Delete.

The morning started fine enough, with Teddy jumping up and down on Dale's stomach to wake him up, and then they had screaming practice for fifteen minutes. Then they researched catapults. Then breakfast, and while they were having breakfast Dale was thinking about how great it was to be up early with Teddy, and he had to make a point of getting up early more often, even when Teddy was with his mom, and then he noticed the microwave clock blinking and that it said 7:15, and now that he thought about it, hadn't he woken up at 7:15? And hadn't they finished screaming practice at 7:15 too?

The short list of approved excuses at Blessed Burgers does not include unreliable electricity. So Dale threw Teddy in the car with his uneaten pancakes stuffed into a sandwich bag and drove him back to Tammy's, and on the way Teddy began to stutter. Dale pointed this out to Tammy, who said she was wondering when he'd get around to noticing his own son had a stutter, and Teddy overheard them talking and starting crying and Tammy said great, now he's full of anxiety and shame because he knows his dad doesn't like the stuttering. And Dale said well nobody *likes* stuttering, he just wanted Teddy to be *normal* was all, and Teddy ran off screaming and Tammy said you just lost yourself another weekend for that remark, Hamburger Man. Plus the support check's late.

Coop was there when he got back in the car. Which was great, and he loves Coop, and it's nice that they're getting close now since he mostly thought of Coop as someone who punched him for no reason every single day of his childhood. But Coop is dead, and he thinks it's not a great thing that they hang out so much these days.

"I could talk to Angel," Coop says now. "If you like, I mean. Smooth things over and whatnot."

"Appreciate it," Dale says. The light's still red. He thinks maybe the driver of the gold Toyota has fallen asleep. Or died. It's nine fifty-three.

He pictures Angel staring at his watch, hand poised above a button marked *Fire Dale*. A weird button to have in the office, ha ha.

"There are other jobs," says Coop. "Gotta remember that, buddy."

"I just want," says Dale, and then he doesn't know what to say. Easier to know what he doesn't want. He doesn't want to lose another job. Doesn't want to be the kind of person who gets fired from a job where he's a dancing hamburger. Doesn't want to let Teddy down again. Doesn't want Teddy to get to the point where he isn't even let down anymore, because he's given up expecting anything from Dale anyway. Doesn't want to start lingering in his own garage, eyeing the antifreeze.

He wants the universe to conspire, just this once, to be merciful. But he suspects maybe that's too much to ask for, suspects maybe it's absolutely a bad idea to ask for that, especially out loud.

The traffic light's red eye stares down at him, unblinking.

Dale imagines there is, somewhere, a cosmic reservoir of goodwill, of plain old good luck. If so, is it doled out at random by the universe, or is there some kind of karmic distribution system at work? He thinks he's been pretty good. Or at least, not evil. It's not as if he's ever done anything really terrible.

"Well," Coop says, "there was the armed robbery."

Damn Lorenzo.

Lorenzo's job is to hang in the entryway of the restaurant dressed as an archangel. He greets customers by flapping his wings and saying, "Welcome to the Paradise of Beef!" When they leave, he says, "Have a Blessed Burger day!" Which doesn't sound so bad, just to hang in the entryway for a few hours every day saying those two things, but the wings have a harness that digs into Lorenzo's torso and cuts off his circulation, and there's a heating vent just below him, so he sweats and chafes all day against the harness, and by the time his shift is over he's soaked in blood and sweat and it's dripping through the costume onto the floor.

Lorenzo had the robbery all worked out. They'd go on a Friday night when Foley was working the register and Angel was sneaking off to his secret girlfriend's house. Foley's too nervous to press the panic button even during drills, and with Foley's wife being pregnant Lorenzo figured he definitely wouldn't be taking any risks. Originally

Fierce Pretty Things

Lorenzo wanted the two of them to dress up as mole rats for the robbery, because he said if they looked like mole rats no one would ever pay attention to their faces or notice any other details. Then he looked up mole rats and said they were pretty horrifying so they'd just wear stockings, as per standard robbery practice.

They bought guns and stockings, and Lorenzo scouted exit routes and considered robbery dates. Dale, meanwhile, imagined terrible things. He figured it would go horribly wrong and the place would end up a scene of carnage. Many dead, with him standing there covered in blood and flesh and ground beef. So he stashed the gun in his car and hoped Lorenzo would just forget the robbery idea entirely. Then Teddy found the gun one day on the way back to Tammy's place and put the barrel in his mouth. Dale took it away, dropped Teddy off, threw up a little, and ended up tossing the gun in the river.

So there's that. That's something good that Dale has done. He has narrowly prevented Teddy from blowing his head off with Dale's gun. Is that the best thing?

The light turns green. The Toyota, amazingly, turns off.

Dale steps on the gas and Coop grabs for a handhold as they shoot forward. Half a mile in two minutes. He can absolutely do this. He says thank you thank you thank you inside his head, and he feels a little like crying. Zooms through the next light, and the next, and it's as if everything is falling into place, as if the universe has just decided it's done fucking with Dale, at least for today.

He makes the turn onto Temple and sees the gates coming down and the lights flashing, hears the train whistle sounding. And he knows right away that the universe hasn't decided not to fuck with Dale. Fucking with Dale is still very much something the universe is going to keep doing, if it's all the same to you. The train, unlike Dale, is *on time*. The universe is actually a little mortified, to be frank, that you'd ask it to derail a train for you, just to get to your little hamburger job.

Dale's car rolls to a stop. He's one block from the restaurant. Above the speeding cars of the train he sees the trees rising up over Vine Street Park.

"Not your fault the train showed up," says Coop. "It's like an act of God, I think, is what I'd argue."

Dale's not thinking about the train. He's thinking about what happened to Teddy's face when Dale said he just wanted Teddy to be normal. Thinking about finding Coop when he came home from school, lying on the floor of the garage in a pile of vomit. Thinking about Angel. It is destiny, yes? It is better this way.

"Not your fault," Coop says again.

At ten o'clock he steps on the accelerator. The engine roars with the car still in neutral, Dale's hand on the gearshift.

"So let's just not be stupid," says Coop.

His eyes are on the trees above the park, sycamores and white oaks that he'd climbed in the days before the antifreeze. Sometimes he played this game in his head as a boy—reach the top and he'd get everything he could ever want. Toys, stacks of gold, a bedroom that looked like a spaceship. To raise the stakes he also imagined terrible things would happen if he didn't make it to the top. He imagined he and everyone he loved would be punished—cursed, condemned to misfortune and unhappiness for all their days. Just a part of the game. Then he'd start to climb, and right away he'd be gripped with anxiety because of the curse he'd invented. When finally and inevitably he would tire, he'd hang from the branches with bloodied fingers, apologizing in his head to everyone he loved for blowing it and allowing misery to be visited upon them all. And then he'd drop like a stone and forget until the next time that he'd so casually and recklessly gambled away everything, every last thing, and lost.

*   *   *

"Park," says Cam, when he sees the sign.

Ruby doesn't answer. She's thinking about how a song can mean one thing because of where you were when you first heard it, how they become entangled, the song and that one thing, and they stay like that for the longest time, mixed up together. So that every time you hear the song again, you kind of have to think about that one thing. Even if it's a horrible thing, and even if it's a beautiful song.

Like, for instance, maybe the song was a park.

Like, for instance, maybe the thing was Uncle Ray. Not really an uncle, Cody used to say. Under his breath but she heard it, and she knew he was saying it to upset her but she didn't get upset. Not really an uncle was okay with her. You couldn't marry an uncle, or run off to an island paradise with an uncle, or even kiss an uncle. And she didn't want to do any of those things, not exactly, not at eleven years old, but she wanted his attention and his affection. Wanted the gifts he brought her—her and Cody both, but always more for her, given in private, delivered with an offhand comment about just stumbling across this little gem and thought of my Ruby, with a wink to contradict the nonchalance and to secretly confirm that yes, the two of them really did share a bond, and who's to say where it might lead them? And where it led them in the end was here, to Vine Street Park. Behind that pavilion right there. Beneath a brilliant sunlit sky. Oh, that sky. It was the sky that finally dashed any doubt she may have had about the rightness or wrongness of the thing, about the low rumbling of thunder in her guts, because what terrible thing could ever happen beneath such a perfect, azure sky?

Anyway it was a long time ago, and Ray was dead. Never told anyone, but happy when he died. Sad that she was happy, that such a thing could make her happy. Wishes sometimes, when she wishes, that she could go back to a time when the sky was only a sky and the park was just a park. Wishes the park could be hers again, without being hers-and-Ray's. Bill tried to take her here once. She said she didn't like parks and he said who doesn't like parks? She said it's just a thing that didn't make any sense about her, and didn't he have anything like that about him? And Bill said yeah, probably he did.

Her phone rings. Ruby looks down, sees the home number.

"Shit," she says. Too late, too late.

"Shit?" says Cam.

And then the old Ghost says, "Glub-glub," and Cam screams in delight and Ruby steps on the gas to keep it from stalling. "Not here," she says, "just please go please please please," and now she can see the traffic light at Temple, and if she doesn't have to stop then maybe she won't stall.

The light turns red. Fuck. Fuck fuck *fuck*. She's barely moving now. Can't step on the brakes or else she's done. She'll have to call Bill and tell him. He's probably already heading out to the shed. He won't get to wake up to the curtains and he won't give her that flinch. Black day coming, Ruby.

The light's red but she doesn't see any cars. Maybe if she just eases through, slow as a bicycle. Maybe just this once.

"Red light," says Cam.

* * *

It goes like this:

There's no sound at all. Just light and heat. And some pain at first, but it's over pretty fast. Dale goes through the windshield at sixty miles an hour, and the worst of the pain is in his head, which splits open in two or three places. One last tiny explosion inside his brain and then he's gone, rising, and he looks down in time to see his body still flying through the air, landing in a heap about a dozen yards away from the crash. A blast of heat pushes him upward, and he spreads his wings to steady himself as he rises above the trees.

Dale looks down, and sees all kinds of things.

Sees Lorenzo, stashing a gun in his locker at work, a new plan already taking shape in his head. Sees Angel on his way to visit his wife in the psychiatric hospital. Sees Coop sailing past him, saying I'm sorry Dale, I'm sorry for punching you all those times for no reason and for drinking the antifreeze and you having to find me on the floor like that. Sees a man in pajamas stomping out to the shed in the backyard, sobbing. Sees Teddy sitting on the floor in his bedroom, surrounded by a protective ring of plastic monsters as the room fills up with sunlight.

Now he sees a woman his age, soaring up from the wreckage. Clawing at the air, trying like mad to get back down to earth, and she looks to Dale like a cartoon bird battling against a hurricane. She screams someone's name over and over, and Dale feels her fury and her helplessness and he understands that there's a boy in the car and she's trying to get back to him, but she won't. The boy is already lost, and this hurts Dale a little more because the boy reminds him of Teddy. And then another blast of heat and smoke comes, and she's gone.

Dale is still rising.

And now he sees Teddy and Tammy, and he's with them both. The three of them are building a catapult, and he loves them and they trust that he loves them. And he's never cruel or impatient or bitter. And every choice he's ever made is the right one, and he's never fucked anything up. And he keeps climbing even when he can't climb any higher, even when his hands are bloodied and everyone has gone home and the last of the daylight has seeped from the sky. He never lets go. He isn't cursed, and no one he loves is cursed. He is a good man, a kind man. And even when he makes mistakes, he fixes them. Before it's too late. Always, please, before it's too late.

*　*　*

Ruby and Cam are halfway through the intersection, and the old Ghost decides it isn't quite done with the world after all and sputters back to life.

Ruby screams, then Cam screams, and then Cam's crazy laugh explodes from the back seat. And Ruby laughs, too, though she doesn't know why. But her son is laughing and the old Ghost is moving, and she thinks okay, yeah.

They round the corner in front of Blessed Burgers and turn onto Temple. No Burger Man, damn.

"Maybe next time," she tells Cam.

"May-bee," he agrees. Maddeningly reasonable now.

They cross the train tracks and come to the next intersection. The light's green and as Ruby glides through she finds another car facing her, stopped under the green light. She slows down but doesn't quite stop, and rolls down the window.

"Need any help?" she calls out, because the light's green and the driver looks a little hypnotized. He's staring up through the windshield at the treetops, lips moving soundlessly. Maybe a lunatic. Or maybe just lost, she thinks. Maybe just a little lost.

"Booger-man," whispers Cam.

"Quiet," Ruby says. She thinks maybe she knows the guy. Hopes he's okay. Hopes for good things for him, whoever he is.

As she rolls past she hollers, "Well have a good day!"

In the back seat, Cam is laughing again.

4

Fierce Pretty Things

I had some fury in me on account of the note I found in study hall so I gave it to Muncie on the way home. He was sitting on the half wall beside the cemetery reading a book, and he didn't see me coming. Muncie was an okay kid. He never stared at the birthmark on my face or said anything about where I lived. I appreciated that but I wasn't in any mood, and there were black flecks at the corners of my eyes and my heart was burning, so I knocked Muncie off the half wall onto the grass behind him, and then I climbed on top and gave it to him. Muncie weighed the same as me but he was soft and easy to knock over. I got him in the stomach a couple times, left-right-left, *sploosh sploosh sploosh* in his flabby gut, and then I knuckled him in both arms and slapped him once in the face. The one to the face wasn't hard but nobody wants to get hit in the face, and that got him crying. I flicked him in the ear for crying. Then I jumped down to the sidewalk and stormed toward Pence's. When I got to Pence's I went straight to the magazine aisle and waited around until Robby behind the counter was looking in my direction. I pulled down the latest issue of *Juggs and Butts* and tucked it in my shirt. Then I grabbed a packet of beef jerky and a box of Dots and stuffed them both in my pockets.

"What," I said, because Robby was looking at me.

"Nothing," he said, and looked away. He was twenty-eight and lived with his mom and his step-dad and his brother Joe, who everybody called Headly because he had water on the brain when he was born and it made his head really big.

"You think I'm stealing your crap?" I said, and I gave him the finger. The beef jerky package fell out of my pocket onto the floor. Robby and I both looked down at it.

"You dropped your jerky, looks like," he said.

"Damn right, you bastard," I said. I picked it up and tore it open and started eating it as I left the store.

A couple minutes later I was okay. I was still on edge but the flecks were gone and my heart was cool, and I had this song going through my head that I play sometimes when I need it—I think of it like there's a record player in there, like the one we had in the house on Old Meadow, and I can just slide the record on whenever I want to hear it, which is a nice thing to be able to do. The song's called "Wild Dog" by Toxic Death Spasm, and it's from their second album, which was the best album they had. It's about this kid named Wild Dog. His mother is a prostitute with a heart of gold, and she gets pregnant and gives birth to Wild Dog in secret because it's against the prostitute rules to have a baby, only someone finds out and kills her and throws the baby out in the garbage. But he's saved by a pack of wild alley dogs, and when he grows up he comes back into town and takes vengeance. The song has some fierce guitar playing, as you'd expect, but my favorite part is when this electric violin comes in toward the end, after Wild Dog finishes up with his vengeance and lights out for the western hills under a gibbous moon. I didn't know what a gibbous moon was, but I liked that violin part. There was something sad and hopeful about that part, like you could imagine Wild Dog maybe sitting down and enjoying some Dots while he rode a railcar under that gibbous moon.

When Roy came home I was sitting outside on the houseboat, listening to the river.

"You give it to anybody today?" he said.

"Ledecky," I said, taking a bite from the beef jerky. "And Muncie."

"Let's go to the Board," he said.

The Board hung on the living room wall next to a bass fishing calendar. Roy swiped it from the office at the factory where he worked and filled it with the names of all the families he remembered from when he was growing up. Some of the names had stars or diamonds next to them that Roy never explained. Others had notes in parentheses right below, things they'd done that Roy remembered, like if somebody called Roy some name when he was six years old, he'd maybe put "(rat boy)" below the name as a reminder. We found Ledecky on the list in the bottom left quadrant. There were three dollar signs after Ledecky's name.

"What's with the dollar signs?"

"Ain't no matter." He pulled a red marker down from above the Board. "You want this one?"

"Go on," I said, and he crossed off Ledecky's name with the marker. Three quarters of the names were crossed off.

"How about Swofford?" Swofford's name was in the middle and it had skulls on both sides, and the skulls had arrows going through their heads. Cole Swofford's family had just moved back to town a few months back. His father owned the Golden Dove Diner and a couple miniature golf places.

"He stays pretty clear of me," I said, and I took a bite of the jerky.

Roy grunted and slid the marker back in place on top of the Board.

Ma took me aside when she started running around with Roy. She said not to be put off by his talk. She said he'd had a rough go of it but it wasn't his fault, or it wasn't completely his fault. He didn't drink so much then and I could see he was good with Ma, so I thought he was okay. When she died he took me aside and said, Well do you want to stay on with me, and I said I guess I did.

"Why'd you give it to Muncie?" he said.

"Ain't no matter," I said.

The note I'd found in study hall said *What's hateful, ugly, and smells like the river?* And there was a drawing of a face with a pig nose and a purple stain on the one side and two fins sticking out the neck.

I went and stretched out on my bed and felt the houseboat swaying around me, and I listened to the river running past and the faint splash of the water against the bedroom wall. Sometimes I liked it, the swaying and the sounds, but today I didn't. I lay there for a bit trying to make the house stop moving with my mind. Usually if I tried hard I could do it, but I couldn't do it now. I rolled onto my stomach and stretched the note out on my pillow and studied it some more. The cursive was really nice, and the tails of all the letters that dropped down low—the g's and the y's and f's—were real extravagant and swirly and impressive. Somebody took a lot of time getting that note to look nice, which almost brought the fury back. I brought the note to the wastebasket and set it on fire and watched it burn until the air smelled like sulfur and catfish. Then I put Toxic Death Spasm on my alarm clock CD player and started paging through *Juggs and Butts*. The girls looked nice but only if you didn't look at their eyes. If you looked at their eyes then you felt kind of bad about it. So I tried to focus on their juggs and their butts the way I was supposed to. But I kept thinking about that note.

Thing is that I knew I was probably ugly, and maybe I did smell like the river even though I couldn't smell it much myself. We'd been in the houseboat, Roy and me, since I was seven. But I didn't like being called hateful. That made me sound like I was rotten, like some fruit that had gone bad. And once something went bad like that, it never got any better.

At dinner Roy said he was going out with his buddy Neal. Most nights he went out with Neal to the Lovejoy, unless Neal was in trouble with his wife and couldn't make it out. When that happened, Roy'd say awful things about Neal for half an hour and then he'd say he was going to walk the river, or he'd say he was taking an extra shift at the quarry. I followed him a couple times and he always ended up at Sign of the Whale, which was on the edge of town near the quarry. I liked the name of that place, Sign of the Whale. It sounded like a secret society, maybe. It sounded like a place where you'd meet up with the resistance and plot to overthrow some alien warlords with horse heads and tentacles. But it was just a dark room with a bar full of old men not looking at each other too much.

"What are you going to do?" he asked.

"Hang out," I said.

"Who with?"

"The boys," I said. I speared a fish stick with my fork and dragged it into a pool of ketchup.

"Probably getting into mischief," he said. "Probably raising some hell in town with the boys. That the plan?"

I looked up and he was smiling, but not at me. He was in a good mood tonight. I said that if mischief came our way, me and the boys wouldn't run from it, and he laughed. He told a story about when he was fourteen, when he and Neal siphoned the gas from all the police cruisers and then threw bricks through the windows of the Dillard's department store. They watched from the shadows and howled as the cops came running on foot all the way from the station.

"One of the top days of my life," he said. "Top five anyways."

I said it sounded like a fine day, and he nodded. But some of the light went out in his face then, and he turned sort of gray. Like he was thinking on how long ago that was, like all the years were rolling over him one after the other and he was trapped under them. Then he took a shuddering breath and he looked like Roy again.

I waited until he was gone and then I stepped out too. It was cool outside but nice enough, and the leaves were falling as the sun was coming down. The cemetery wasn't far. Ma was on the back side on account of her being a suicide. You went in through a little iron gate covered in ivy, and then you went up a hillside facing north, out of the sun, so it always felt cooler there than anywhere else. You could hear the river running when you were up there too. I set down my backpack by her marker, under the branches of a twisted white oak.

"Things are okay," I said. I liked to say that straight away, just so she was in the right frame of mind and didn't think I was in any kind of trouble or anything.

It's good to see you again and you're looking taller, she said. Or she didn't really say that, but I could hear it well enough in my head. I could picture her too. In my head she was lying on one of the oak branches

Fierce Pretty Things

right over my head, and she looked like a cherub you'd see in an old painting, all chubby arms and puffy cheeks and a young pink face and curly brown hair that fell down to cover her bosom. She was too skinny when she was alive—I was only six at the time so mostly I remember her from pictures, but I knew she was too skinny. So I liked thinking of her as one of them cherubs.

I told her I'd gotten a B-minus on an essay I wrote about Saturn, and she said that was a fine thing and asked me if there were some interesting facts I read about when I was learning on Saturn, and I said yes there were. I told her about how each year on Saturn is like thirty years here on Earth because of how long it takes for it to go around the sun. So that means you'd only be a little over a year old on Saturn by now, I said, and I could tell she liked that, her being just a baby in Saturn years.

Then I told her I'd given it to Muncie on the way home.

She was quiet for a bit. Then she said, *I guess he had it coming is what you're saying.*

"Well, maybe he did," I said, sort of defensive because of her tone. "It's hard to say for sure exactly."

I'm sure it was Muncie who wrote that note, then, with all those swirls and flourishes.

I hadn't told her about the note, which made the hairs on my arms stand up. I said the point was that it could've been Muncie. There wasn't any way to know. And if I didn't stand up for myself then nobody ever would. I said it was about balancing the ledger, which was something I'd heard Roy say.

I'm sure that's right, she said.

I sat there holding my knees against my chest. It was just about full dark. I cleared my throat and said, "Tomorrow I think I'll do better." She didn't say anything to that, so I went on. "There's no reason I can't do better tomorrow. I'm not some damn fruit that you need to throw away."

It was dead quiet and I could hear the river running, far off. I said I needed some space and walked down along the water. When I got back to the houseboat I set up a lantern on the deck rail and fished for a while in the dark. There was a cool wind blowing and there wasn't anything wrong with being on the river that I could see, but I was troubled. I felt like I was Wild Dog himself, and I played the violin solo on the record player in my head, but that didn't fix it. Finally I reached into my bag and took out the plastic hand I lifted from a Dillard's mannequin a while back. In the dark it looked real enough. I ran the plastic fingers through my hair a couple times. Nobody could see me, and there wasn't anything wrong with it except that I'd lifted it from Dillard's, which Roy told me was basically run by criminals.

There's maybe something wrong with it, Ma said, in my head. *But you're okay.*

Next day I gave it to Hoyle in the locker room, but only because he made a sniffing noise when I walked by. I knuckled him in the back of the head, and Kaminsky the gym teacher saw it and gave me detention, probably because Kaminsky was a Pole and had a grudge against Roy on account of Roy being German and Germany invading Poland back in the day. I didn't mind the detention because I could just sit in my regular seat by the window and write out the lyrics to Toxic Death Spasm songs until it was over, and Graves, who was the shop teacher and always got stuck with me in detention, was afraid of me and left me pretty well alone.

But when I got into detention the room wasn't empty. There was a girl sitting by the window right behind my regular seat. Her head was down and she was writing something in her notebook. That upset me but I didn't know what I could do about it, so I signed in with Graves and looked around the room trying to figure out where I'd sit. I could see the black flecks coming on and Graves was watching me with a nervous look.

"Christ Jesus, Graves, I'm fine," I said. And I went to my regular seat.

The girl didn't look up. Her hair was long and dark and tangled and it kept her face hidden, but I knew who it was. It was Franny. She'd moved to town over the summer. I hadn't ever talked to her and we didn't have any classes together but I'd seen her walking sometimes, and there weren't many new people who moved into town. She was living a few houses down from where we used to live on Old Meadow.

I sat down and pulled out my notebook and started in on "Wild Dog," trying to write the letters all Gothic-like and extra grim. But

Fierce Pretty Things

I only got as far as *One black night in the heart of Mississippi* when I stopped because I heard her breathing behind me.

"You got to breathe so damn loud?" I said, turning my face toward the window so she could hear me.

"I got a right to breathe," she said.

"I can't concentrate is all," I said.

She said, "What's so special that you need concentrating for?"

I thought of calling her a rotten whore but I didn't, because I was remembering my promise to Ma and I was thinking about being a bad fruit. I went back to my notebook.

"You're tapping your foot now," I said.

"I'm a dancer," she said. "I can't help it. I tap sometimes."

"Maybe that's why you're in here," I said. "Because you can't help tapping your damn foot."

"Maybe you're a dummy," she said.

I about snapped my pen in half then. I said, "Damn, why'd you have to sit here anyway?"

"Why'd you?" she said. "I was here first anyways."

"You're giving me the black flecks," I said, clenching my fists.

That finally made her look up, and I saw her face. Beneath all that wild hair she was fierce pretty, with a face that was kind of dirty and eyes greener than anything I ever saw.

"What's that mean?"

I shook my head. I didn't want to explain. Instead I looked down at her notebook, and I saw she'd drawn a picture of a family. Only they were all skeletons. A dad skeleton and a mom skeleton holding hands, and a little girl skeleton with a red hair ribbon tied around her skull.

"That's weird," I said.

"You're weird." She flipped the page over so I couldn't see it anymore. On the next page there was some writing she'd done. It was upside down but I could see that it was in cursive. It was fine handwriting too. All the letters with tails that dropped down—the *g*'s and the *y*'s and the *f*'s—were extravagant and swirly too.

"Maybe I am," I said. I set my jaw tight and I said, "Maybe I'm just somebody who's rotten and ugly and smells like the river." And everything was black then.

She blinked at me. "You're Vardy," she said.

I thought, then, of all the hateful things I wanted to say to her. I thought of calling her names, names that would sting her and that she'd keep with her for a long time, until she was older, until she was an old woman looking back on her days. She'd be a grandmother with all this history behind her, with a husband who was long dead and kids who had grown up and had kids themselves, and she'd have lots of good times to look back on. She'd be in some old retirement home with flowers on the windowsill and photographs everywhere, and on every holiday she'd get loads of holiday cards because of how much she was loved. Her eyes would still be green like they were now too. But now and then she'd look back over her life, because that's what you do when you're old, and she'd find me there. She'd remember the time she came face to face with me, and the things I said. And those things would hurt her all over again. That's all I'd be, then. Just something rotten waiting in her mind when she looked back, to make her feel bad as she closed in on the grave.

My gut hurt and it felt like something was broken in me. I didn't say anything at all. I only turned my head and went back to my Wild Dog lyrics.

When detention was over, I heard her get up behind me but I didn't lift my head. I waited until she was gone, and then I stood up and grabbed my backpack. As I turned around I saw she'd left a note on the desk.

I'm sorry they asked me to write that because they liked my handwriting and I wanted them to like it but I was wrong to do it. Nobody knows anything about anybody. Franny.

* * *

After detention I went to Pence's and lifted another magazine and another box of Dots. It was raining some by the time I left the store but I didn't care. I had the note from Franny folded in my back pocket.

Nobody else was outside and I liked that. I liked being the only one walking the streets, like it was a mutant apocalypse. I opened the Dots and shook a few into my mouth, wishing Will was still around. Will would've appreciated the way the sky looked, and the empty streets and all. You never met anyone as smart as Will. He designed a trebuchet that we built to defend the town against mutants who were plotting on the east bank to swim across and eat our brains. I thought we ought to launch a preemptive strike in the black of night, but Will said we had to wait for an actual attack. He said we could fire test rounds into the water as a show of force, though, and so we did, and I agreed that was damned satisfying even if we didn't end up slaughtering any mutants. We fell out of friendship, I guess, and he moved away a couple years back. I ran into him coming home from school the day before he moved, and I asked if he remembered that damn trebuchet and he said of course he remembered. I said it's a shame things are like this, and he asked what I meant, and I said I didn't know but I thought it was a shame anyhow.

I'd walked all the way to the old neighborhood without thinking about it, and I was soaking wet. Somehow I ended up in front of Franny's house. It was getting dark but there weren't any lights on in the main part of the house, only the blue-white glow from a TV in the living room behind the curtains. I didn't want to be a creeper but I stood there for a little while longer. Just wondering what it was like in there. I pictured the family sitting around and watching some movie together, Franny and her parents. They probably had a bowl of popcorn and some other snacks, too, like Junior Mints, or maybe some kind of homemade movie snack that only they knew about. They probably even had some great name for it that wouldn't make sense to anyone else, like snowbear necklaces. Which would be like Gummy bears dipped in white chocolate and then attached to a string so you could wear them and eat them at the same time. Probably Franny's mom made the necklaces in the morning and kept them in the fridge. And then at night the three of them would sit on the couch together even though there were other chairs they could use, and they'd throw a blanket over themselves and watch the movie, and now and then one of them would take a bite from the snowbear necklace, not even thinking about it. Sometimes they'd have to slide the necklace around to get the next set of snowbears in line, but they wouldn't think about that either because this was just part of the regular routine for the three of them.

I saw someone get up from the couch then, just a silhouette behind the curtain but I guessed it was Franny. She moved to the center of the room and raised her arms up over her head, hands pointing together, and she did a kind of slow ballerina spin. She did a few more moves that looked pretty nice, too, and then it looked like she took a bow toward the couch. *That was great ballerina dancing, Franny,* they were probably saying to her then, *now why don't you come back and sit down and have a couple more snowbears.*

At dinner I told Roy I'd gotten detention for giving it to Hoyle.

He said Hoyle wasn't even on the Board, and I said well he ought to be. I said also it wasn't some kind of big deal but I met a girl named Franny when I was in detention. "She drew a picture of a skeleton family that was pretty nice," I said. "She has green eyes and her hair's sort of wild, and she's a dancer too."

"And?" he said.

"And I don't know."

"You think she likes you."

My face heated up some. "Nobody said anybody likes anybody."

"Sounds like somebody does."

"It's not like that," I said.

"Just don't get your hopes up, is all," he said. "Better you don't expect anything too fine from the world is the thing."

I said I knew that. I asked him if he was going out with Neal.

"Neal is a coward and a son of a bitch," he said. "I might do another shift tonight, though."

After dinner I put on my boots and went up see Ma. The rain was still coming but it was dry enough under the big oak. I shone a flashlight on the marker and told her about Franny and said I felt better than I had in a while, and I wasn't sure why. I said I didn't want that feeling to go away but I wasn't sure what I could do to keep that from happening.

So what am I supposed to say to that? she said.

I said I didn't know, but maybe she could just be encouraging and cherublike.

Hell with cherubs, she said. *Who said you deserve to feel anything as good as that? Who said anyone deserves that?*

"Didn't say I deserve it," I told her. "Just want it, is all."

Fierce Pretty Things

Then maybe don't be a hateful rotten fruit boy, she said, and she wouldn't say anything else after that. Sometimes she was like that.

I went home and listened to music, and then I turned out the lights and lay in bed, running my fingers across the hand from Dillard's and looking up at the glow-in-the-dark crucifix on the wall above my bed. It was Ma's crucifix. I found it in a box and Roy hadn't wanted it, so I'd hung it on the wall between two Toxic Death Spasm posters. It spooked me during the day, seeing Jesus all bloodied and hanging on the cross like that, but at night you couldn't see the cross at all, only Jesus's glow-in-the-dark body. So it looked like He was floating up there, like He was free and hovering with outstretched arms over all the bastards who nailed Him up there. Untouched by all that. I stared up at Him and thought about what Franny wrote, about how nobody knew anything about anybody. Then I fell asleep and dreamed I was driving one of the nails into His hands, and I said, Hold still you dummy kike, and Franny was there, except she was only a skeleton girl with a red hair ribbon. Her skeleton head was tilted down and she looked full of sorrow to me just because of the way her skull was hanging. Ma was in the dream, too, only she was behind a door and all I could hear was the faucet running and all I could see was the light under the door, but I knew she was cutting herself open in there. I woke up and listened to the rain pounding on the windows for a long time until the sun came up.

In the morning I made up my mind not to give it to anybody. So when I came out of the locker room for gym and I saw Hoyle talking with Stacy Adams by the chin-up bar and they both looked over at me and she laughed at something he said, probably something like *Don't look now but fish boy Vardy is coming by so keep your worms in your pocket*, I kept my hands by my sides and tried out a smile as I walked by.

"Nobody's stealing anybody's worms here," I said.

They both smiled back at me, but when I walked past I could see Hoyle out of the corner of my eye, spinning his finger around his temple, which made Stacy Adams giggle. He didn't have to do that. I thought I wasn't going to have any choice except to give it to him. Then I pictured skeleton Franny looking on wearing her red hair ribbon as I drove Hoyle's head into the bleachers and knuckled him until his head caved in, and my gut hurt again all of a sudden. So all I did was keep smiling, and I started whistling some of the violin solo from "Wild Dog" as I walked away. I didn't feel great about that. But I didn't feel totally rotten either. I felt like half rotten.

Thanks Vardy, Franny said, in my head I mean. *That's something good in you that you just showed.*

I kept to myself and tried not to get into conversations or listen to anyone. I figured that was a way to stay out of trouble. When I was between classes I even pictured Jesus hovering in the hallway, bobbing this way and that over all the kids with His arms spread wide, and glowing from head to toe. Free of all pain and worry.

"You and me, Vardy," He said. "We're like two peas in a pod."

"Yessir," I agreed.

A couple times I passed Franny between periods. I was hoping she'd make eye contact but she didn't. I wanted to tell her it was okay what she'd done, writing that note. I didn't blame her for that. I even wrote her a note myself when I was sitting at lunch, but I didn't know what to say in it, so I just wrote some stuff about Toxic Death Spasm and about Will's trebuchet and about the sound of the water splashing against the houseboat. Then I read it over and decided nobody wanted to hear about those things, and I didn't know why I wrote them in the first place.

The only bad time was when I saw Headly after lunch, at his locker. Headly had grown a beard over the summer so his head wouldn't look as big as it did on his shoulders. Otherwise he looked normal enough, but he was always talking to himself and smiling at nothing at all, like he was doing now. He was stroking his beard, too, and that set me off.

"What the hell are you smiling about and stroking your beard for, Headly?" I said to him.

He smiled back at me but his eyes were off in the corner somewhere.

"There's nothing funny going on for fuck's sake," I said to him. That made him laugh, so I raised my fist, and Headly cowered down like a little boy, covering his damn face with his hands and giggling, and that set me off even more. "Jesus Christ, you think I'm really going to hit somebody like you, Headly," I said. But he was crying by then so

Fierce Pretty Things

I only stomped off, feeling bad about everything. I felt like everything I'd done was falling apart.

When classes were over I walked back to my locker. Somebody had sprayed a fish on the locker door with white spray paint. It had whiskers like a catfish and the bottom jaw jutted out a bit. I thought it was probably a flathead catfish. I looked around and saw Swofford and Hoyle standing across the hall by their lockers, yapping about something, probably about how good a joke it was since flathead catfish are so damn big and ugly, and Hoyle was probably saying we should've put a wine stain on its face too somehow, and Swofford was probably saying, Now that's an idea, Hoyle, and next time we'll do exactly that, and next thing I had Swofford by the neck pinned against the locker and he was turning bright red, and I screamed in Swofford's face that we didn't even have flathead catfish in this part of the state and he was a fucker who didn't know anything about catfish and nobody cared about his golden boy smile anyway. Then Swofford started crying himself and said he'd never done anything to me before and what the hell was I doing, and everyone was looking at us now, and even Franny was there, and Jesus floated by with his outstretched arms and He said, "Go on and bash his head in. You know you want to do it. We aren't any two peas in a pod, Vardy. Just go on and do it."

I didn't say it but I thought He was a bastard for saying that to me. But I let go of Swofford's neck and he slid down the locker. I had the black flecks again and it was hard for me to see straight but I made myself say, "I'm sorry, Swofford, there's no call for that." I looked over at Franny to see if maybe she'd have a kind look on her face for me, for saying that. I searched her face but I couldn't tell if it was a kind expression she was wearing. But I imagined she was thinking, *Now that couldn't have been easy to stop from giving it to Swofford right there, so I appreciate you doing that. Me and Jesus and your Ma, we all do.*

Then I turned back to Swofford, who'd climbed to his feet, and he socked me in the jaw.

I was off balance and went down hard, and he was on top of me then, pinning me down with his legs and whaling on my shoulders and my gut and my face, too, and I heard the other kids hooting and screaming, and I searched for Franny and she was looking down at me with her head cocked to one side, like she was trying to figure out if I was for real or not. I wanted her to know that I was for real so I took Swofford's beating and didn't try to stop him. He was red-faced and his perfect hair was all crazy and he just kept raining down punches on me. He was still crying too. Blood from my nose and my lip was splattered on the floor by my face. Pretty soon Graves came over and put a stop to everything, and by the time I looked up again Franny was gone.

"I hope you ran into a brick wall," Roy said when I came home. He had a Ziploc bag full of ice and was holding it against my face. "I hope that's the explanation for what I'm seeing."

"Swofford gave it to me," I said.

"Jesus," he said. "Oh sweet Jesus."

"I'm tired of it," I said. "I don't want to be who I am anymore."

"Welcome to the club," he said. "Maybe you can decide that after you give it to Swofford next time." Then he went to the Board to add a star next to the skulls by Swofford's name.

Later I went by Franny's place. The moon was shining bright and her lights were off like they always were except for the television set. The living room curtains were drawn. Franny was dancing again, only this time it looked like her mom and dad were standing off to one side, watching her. Her dad was wearing a hat and her mom had a bonnet on. Franny danced over to them and she grabbed her dad's hand and he leaned down like he was dipping her real low, and then she danced away.

The next day I was still banged up, and my eye was about swollen shut. I thought everyone was looking at me different. I thought maybe they'd decided I wasn't so rotten, since I'd taken a beating from Swofford like that. Maybe they were angry with Swofford. Maybe he was getting those looks now, the looks where they'd pretend they weren't looking at you at all, like their eyes just flitted right past you, and maybe they'd turn down the wrong hallway just to avoid going past you. I felt a little bad for Swofford about that. And I thought it wouldn't be the craziest thing in the world if we ended up being friends, Swofford and me. Then I'd have to tell Roy, and Roy would get all worked up about it. But eventually Roy would be okay with it. Maybe he'd even take the Board down. We'd have a little ceremony, and Roy would say something that was surprising and made you cock your head and wonder what he had in him. Because nobody knows anything about anybody.

I left first period and I was thinking about the ceremony—I thought maybe we'd set the Board adrift on the river and shoot flaming arrows into it at midnight, if Roy would let us—when I turned the corner and saw Swofford and Hoyle.

"Swofford," I said, nodding at them both. "Hoyle."

"Fish boy," Hoyle said, and held his nose.

"Now, damn," I said. "You don't got to do that."

"That's right," Swofford said. "Leave fish boy alone. He's got feelings."

"Fish feelings," said Hoyle. And he puffed out his cheeks like a blowfish.

I was full of meanness then but I kept it down and walked away.

"You thought it'd be easy," Jesus said, popping up behind Hoyle's shoulder, outstretched arms glowing fierce and green. "Does it look easy, fruit boy?"

"Damn, I didn't say it looked easy," I said. "Who the hell said that?"

The day didn't get much better. Twice I was tripped in the hallways, and both times I landed hard and it took the wind out of me, and when I looked up kids were staring at me, waiting to see what I'd do. I wanted them to see I wasn't going to do anything, so then they'd stop worrying about me and stop saying things about me and look at me the same way they looked at everybody else.

The second time I was tripped, Franny was there. She squatted down and said, "What are you doing anyways?"

"I got a plan," I said.

"Seems dumb, whatever it is," she said.

"I'm improving myself," I said. I sat up against the locker and blinked at her with my good eye.

"You don't look improved is the thing."

"Maybe," I said, "we could meet up later. Just walk around or whatnot."

"I can't," she said.

"Because you got to go off and watch movies and eat snowbears," I said, angry.

"What are you talking about?"

"I don't know."

"Don't be an idiot," she said. She was close enough then that I could smell her shampoo. It smelled like strawberries and wood smoke.

Later in study hall, I found another note on the floor. The note said, *Vardy's getting what's coming to him after school.*

"Now what are you gonna do?" Jesus asked, when I was standing at my locker.

"Thinking on it," I said.

That wasn't fully true. I guess I'd been thinking on it but I hadn't come up with anything. I was tired and didn't have any damn idea about what to do, and I thought I was bound to let everybody down.

When school was done I went out to see what was coming.

Kids were out there milling around, dozens of them, standing on the front lawn by the flagpole or blocking the sidewalks in each direction. There was a buzz in the air too, everybody talking low, but the buzz died as soon as I stepped out.

In the middle of it all was Swofford.

"I thought we were done with things," I said, coming up to him.

"You thought we were done," he said. "You think you can just say when something is done?" And he slapped me in the face.

I looked around for Franny but I couldn't find her. Jesus was there, hovering by the flagpole, but He was silent now, waiting to see what I'd do.

"We ought to just shake hands," I said.

Swofford slapped me in the face again, and my eyes teared up.

"Goddamn," I said. "You're making it hard for us to become best friends, Swofford." My eyes were stinging and I looked all around me. And what I saw was that everyone was just waiting for Swofford to give it to me. They didn't care if I fought back or not. And when I looked at their faces I could remember something vicious I'd done to each of them.

"Swofford," I said. "I don't know what to do here."

He threw me down then, and a big cheer went up. I put my hands over my face but otherwise I didn't do anything to stop it. A couple other kids joined in, Hoyle and Sherman and Ledecky and even Stacy Adams, kicking me in the legs while Swofford pummeled me in the stomach and the chest. I turned my head on the grass and I could see Franny up on the top step by the school entrance. I wondered if she was going to run down to stop them, maybe make some kind of speech about how we were all in this together, about how I deserved a second chance just like anybody else would. But she only turned and went back into the shadows of the school, and then I took a punch to the face. I turned my head to see who it was and it was Muncie. He smiled and called me a demon son of a bitch and punched me again.

It went on like that for a couple minutes. I knew I'd be floating above it like Jesus sometime soon, without any pain, but it was taking a good while.

"You got it all wrong," Jesus said, looking down on me between punches. "You think there aren't any damn nails up here just because you don't see 'em glowing?"

After a time I did start to float. I looked down and saw the mess I was. I saw how big I looked, like a monster dragged down at last by the villagers, and I saw how happy they all were. My things had spilled from my bag onto the grass, and I watched Muncie reach down to pick up Ma's hand from Dillard's. He held it over his head and they all shrieked and cheered, and then he smashed it down on the sidewalk and broke it into a hundred pieces, and they cheered even harder.

Sometime later I drifted back down. Everything ached at least a little, but nothing hurt more than anything else so I figured I was okay. I looked around for Franny but I didn't see her. Then I saw black boots coming my way. I rolled over and squinted up at the afternoon sun.

"Headly," I said.

He was smiling. And I knew for sure he was going to reach down to help me up. We'd put our arms around each other and it would be something good, something small but good, and it would teach me a lesson about something. We wouldn't even have to say anything or make any big speeches. It would just be something true that we both knew.

Then he lifted his boot.

I said, "Okay, Headly," as his boot came down.

*   *   *

When I came to, there was a note crumpled in my hand. *I waited as long as I could to see if you were ok. Come to my house. Franny.*

It was growing dark by then. The streetlamps were coming on as I turned onto Old Meadow. I stopped in front of Franny's place, swaying back and forth in the wind. The television wasn't on tonight, and all the lights were off except for an upstairs bedroom. I went to the door and found another note in Franny's writing, telling me to come in without knocking. I pushed open the door and stepped inside.

The living room was dark and cool, and I made my way through the shadows toward the bottom of the stairs. On the way I passed a hat rack with a fedora perched on top. Next to the hat rack was an ironing board wearing a bonnet. I kept going and went up the stairs.

In the bedroom I found Franny, sitting in an armchair next to a hospital bed set up in the middle of the room.

"She can't hear you, it's okay." She waved me over. "You won't bother her. But she likes having me next to her. She's my aunt. You can't tell now but she was some kind of beauty. I can't get her makeup right, though."

I looked at the woman in the bed. I could see that she'd been a beauty, once. "Can I sit with her too?" I asked.

"You should," she said.

So I brought a chair over and sat with the two of them. The window was open a bit and there were sounds coming in, cars going past and leaves scraping on the sidewalk and some other sound, too, something low and forceful that I couldn't make out.

What I was thinking of, sitting there, was just Franny. How she'd dance in the living room. I pictured her doing her ballerina spins in the glow of the television, with the hat rack and the ironing board propped up against the wall. I imagined the whisper of her feet as she moved along the floor. Trying not wake up her aunt. Bowing after she was

Fierce Pretty Things

done. Thank you. Why, thank you. And I don't know why but it made me think of Roy, too, and the Board. All of it was running together in my head. And through it all the low sound I was hearing only got louder still. I knew it was the river I was hearing, moving past in the dark, far off.

I stayed for a while, only listening.

When I left I walked to the cemetery. It was cooler now and the wind was picking up. Leaves were blowing across the back hillside and something was going on with my heart but I didn't understand what it was. I thought maybe I'd gotten hit harder than I knew and I was all bruised up in there.

Up ahead I saw someone at Ma's grave. He was lying on the ground with his legs curled up to his chest. The light had fallen but I could just make out the green army jacket. I stopped then. I turned and looked down the hill, toward where I knew the river was. It's a slow river but in my head the water was rushing like mad, like something fierce and relentless. I thought the right thing for me to do then was to go down the hill and leave Roy to himself. He didn't want anyone to see him curled up like that. Nobody wanted to be seen like that.

But I didn't go back down. I kept hearing the river in my head, and the wind was blowing, and I didn't know a damn thing about what to do. So I turned up the hill and made my way toward him as the night closed in.

5

Scarecrows

They're in Dixon's yard again. A boy and a girl, both blond-haired and tanned even though it's late March and the ground is covered in snow. They're dancing around the wooden scarecrows in the corner of the fenced yard.

Maude comes by on her way to fold the laundry, basket tucked against her hip. She stops and puts one hand on the back of Dixon's wheelchair and peers out the window. "What are you looking at?"

"Nothing, nothing," he says.

"Really."

"The snow," he says, with a vague, wobbly-armed gesture toward the glass. The girl's doing cartwheels now across the snowy yard. The

Post-it note that Dixon found inside his medicine cabinet, in Dixon's shaky handwriting, says, IT'S MOLLY. SHE WAS FIFTY-THREE WHEN SHE DIED.

Weird. Well, okay, the whole thing is weird. He doesn't know why Molly is a young girl again. She looks to be eleven or twelve. And yet. The dimples, the sea-green eyes, the toothy smile—it has to be Molly.

"I'm sick of the snow," says Maude.

The boy, now. Molly's brother. Dixon has been trying to remember his name, but it's been so long. THE BOY—STARTS WITH A B. PROBABLY! Infuriating. Brian? Bradley? Barry? He was nine, Dixon thinks. But he looks younger out there in the yard. Insubstantial. A string bean of a boy. As Dixon watches, the string bean bows gravely in his direction, then turns back toward the yard. He raises his thin arms in a martial arts posture, preparing to face off against some invisible opponent across the yard. Then he moves forward, executing a series of wild but entertaining punches, double punches, leaps, blocks, and lunges. Halfway across, he tries an ambitious spinning leg kick and goes down in the snow just as Molly wipes out on her cartwheel, landing behind him.

Dixon puts his hand over his chest. The slightest pressure there.

Maude turns from the window. "Chest?"

"Indigestion," he says.

She makes an unhappy *mmmph* sound. "The hip?"

When Dixon hesitates, she goes to the kitchen and gets a laminated strip eighteen inches wide, showing faces in various stages of horror on a one-to-ten scale. Dixon points to the face in the sixth position, which is shaded orange and has a squiggly horizontal line for the mouth.

"You always say six."

"I'm fine, Maude."

"You're pale."

"I'm old."

Outside, Molly and B spring up from the snow, arms raised triumphantly, and Dixon hides a smile.

Maude sets down the basket and folds her arms over her chest. She narrows her eyes. "Don't," she says.

"I'm not seeing things," Dixon says.

"I can't," Maude says. "Not today."

The two kids are now linked arm in arm in the middle of the yard. B wiggles his free arm like a spaghetti noodle, starting a wave that moves across his body like a shiver. Through his small chest, out the shoulder, then down his other arm and into Molly, who executes the same move in reverse, completing the wave by blowing Dixon a delightful, snowy kiss.

"You've got a look," Maude says.

Dixon turns away from the window. "It's my face. I get looks," he says. "I'm—"

"Old, I know."

He wants to tell her. It kills him not to tell her. He wants to say, Maude, you've got to see them, they're perfect! They've got the most beautiful faces and they're happy, Maude! (Well, mostly happy. Sometimes when he looks closely, he might see that B's fine hair is damp, matted against his forehead. That one of Molly's green eyes doesn't blink, or has grown muddy and dull. That B's feet are webbed, or that he has no feet at all, only rootlike tendrils snaking down from his calves, affixing him to the earth. It's only late in the day when he sees these things, though, and they're easily forgotten.)

But the Post-it note was clear. DO NOT TELL MAUDE. That one was stuck to the inside of his bedside drawer when he went to retrieve his glasses. Then there was the other one, folded and tucked inside the pocket of Dixon's robe. DON'T EVEN THINK ABOUT IT. STOP. NO.

The notes are a new thing. He's almost positive that they're a new thing. He's had trouble remembering, and the notes help. Maude thinks it's the drugs causing him to forget, but it goes back a few years, since before Dixon's last heart attack. He was better at hiding the lapses then. The broken hip—and the complications from the broken hip, and the painkillers, and the side effects from the painkillers—have only made things worse. He has a vague sense—but everything is a vague sense these days—that he's forgotten much more than he realizes. Details small and large. The boy's name, for example. So when an old memory surfaces, jewel-like, from the dark waters of his mind, he tries to make a note of that too.

Fierce Pretty Things

Maude goes to fold the laundry, squeezing his shoulder lightly as she departs.

He's told her about the kids already. About the ghosts. That has to be it. Explains the Post-it notes. He has a memory, fuzzy around the edges, sharp and unhappy in the center, of Maude's face going slack, of Maude looking dead-eyed and broken while Dixon blathers on.

And he gets it. He totally and completely gets it. The boy's name is hidden from him, but Dixon remembers the day he and Maude went to select the casket. The funeral director suggested a silver one. It had a spray of doves against a field of baby blue on the inside panel, above the words *Going Home*. "My son doesn't need to look up at birds when he's dead," Maude told him. She said her son had no use for birds when he was alive, and even less use for them now. Fuck your goddamn birds, she said. On the way home the radio was playing "Me and Bobby Mc-Gee" by Janis Joplin, and the wind was blowing orange and yellow leaves across the road, and Maude cried like a little girl.

Dixon shifts in the wheelchair, getting comfortable. Molly looks good. Nice to see her with her long hair again. He thinks about Maude, how she knitted a cap when the adult Molly—still with the dimples and the sea-green eyes—was going through radiation. Knitted eighteen caps, actually. *I know you didn't need eighteen caps*, Maude told her in the hospital toward the end. That killed him. The past tense. He wanted to tell Maude to take it back, to take back that past tense. *I needed*, said Molly, *exactly eighteen*. And they smiled at each other, the two of them. Dixon sobbed. The two women were fine, but Dixon sobbed.

"Looking good, Mol," he says, but quietly. No reason to upset Maude. Molly blows him another kiss, and then the kids approach each other. They clasp hands as their bodies meet, chest to chest and cheek to cheek. They tango their way to Dixon's window, eyes shining and faces playfully serious. At the edge of the patio—they never come closer than the patio—they execute a turn, a surprisingly good one considering that they're kids, and they're dead, and they're in the snow. He can see them begin to giggle as their faces turn away. They dance to the garden, now buried under the snow except for the tops of the two scarecrows in the corner. When they reach the corner, they fade into nothing, and then they're gone.

Later, lying on his side and facing the wall while Maude cleans him up, Dixon says, "Hey, Maude."

"Uh-huh," she says.

"We should take tango lessons."

"Turn just a little," sighing.

"I always loved the tango, Maude."

"More. Turn more. I can't lift your whole body, Dixon."

He turns. "So graceful, so powerful, Maude. Like a love story. Like the whole arc of a love story in a single dance."

"Ah," she says, and she stops.

"Maude?"

"It's just," she says.

"Oh." Dixon's chest fills for a moment. And there is it, another jewel breaking the surface. This one is dark and ruby red, the color of Maude's dress, Maude's lips, the flush in her face as he pulls her young, graceful body to his.

"I forgot, Maude."

"Not your fault, Dixon." But she sounds tired.

"Maude," he says, thinking of something. Something that's just occurred to him. "Our boy, his name is on the tip of my tongue, but I can't—"

"No," she says, sharply. "Just—no. Not again." And then she's silent.

DON'T BRING UP THE BOY ANYMORE. The problem with the Post-it note scheme, Dixon keeps forgetting, is that it's so easy for him to forget about the Post-it note scheme.

When she's finished, she helps him back into the wheelchair. He can walk a bit, though unsteadily; the wheelchair, in Dixon's mind, is mostly to keep her from worrying that he'll do something stupid. In January he tried to shovel the sidewalk while Maude was taking a nap. Dumb, dumb. But he hated seeing Maude do it. He didn't get far. She found him in the driveway, face down, lip bloodied and bruises all along one side of his face. Nothing too bad. But of course he looked frightful. Scared Maude to death. She sat in the garage by herself for half an hour after they got home from the hospital. Said she just needed a few.

Fierce Pretty Things

"Time for your Demerol," she says.

She reaches for a pill, and Dixon sees a shadow on her face. He leans forward to inspect her. When she raises her eyes to him, she's different. A haggard old woman! Right in his house! Handing him a pill, of all things. Expecting him to not even notice!

"Clever," he says, and he swats the pill out of her hand.

She looks hurt for a second. Hurt and confused. *Foiled.* Exactly the way he imagines that a murderess would look. Then she scoops the pill up from the carpet and stands up straight.

"Dixon," she says.

"I know my name," he says. He's shaking a little now. "My name— *my* name—isn't the mystery here."

"Let's not do this."

"Oh, that's fine. That's fine coming from you. *Let's not do this.*" He's still shaking. Just a bit of drool happening, too, but that's fine. The good news is that he's figured it out in time. "Taking advantage of me," he says, "because I'm in this wheelchair."

"I'm not doing anything of the kind. And you know it."

"When Maude gets home she'll take care of you. You think you can pull one over on Maude? That woman can *move.* She'll dance around you like a—" He stops, trying to pull something free from the dark waters. Something he just had. "Hold on, hold on." Oh, and there it is. It's red. It's ruby red. "She could—here's what she could do. *The tango.*" He smiles, full of grim satisfaction. "You're going to mess with a woman who can do the *tango*? There's a whole love story in a tango, you know." The pressure in his chest builds again. "A whole—a whole arc, is what I mean. Hold on. Let me just—I want to think for a minute."

She sits down at the table and puts her hands on her knees and waits.

Dixon watches her for a few seconds. He watches how her face changes, becomes familiar, becomes more than familiar.

"Hey," he says. He touches her hand. "Hey, Maude. Hey."

She opens her eyes. Still a beauty, Maude. She says, "Listen, Dixon. How about you take your pill?"

He takes the pill from her. She watches him put it in his mouth, then hands him a glass of water.

Scarecrows

"Dixon," she says, "I have to run out. Just to refill some prescriptions."

"Okay," he says.

"Maybe you can take a nap while I'm gone. You must be tired."

"I guess I'm a little tired."

"You want me to help you into bed?"

Dixon smiles at her. "I'll sit here, Maude. I'll sit by the window if that's okay."

When she leaves, he removes the pill from under his tongue and drops it into a baggy in his pocket. He takes out the pad and writes, MAUDE LOVED TO DANCE. WE USED TO DO THE TANGO. SHE WORE A RED DRESS. He rolls himself into the bedroom, sticks the note inside the top drawer of his dresser, then rolls into the bathroom, where he writes a second note. Apologizing. Just in case he forgets that he upset her. At least she'll know he was sorry. He can't remember exactly what he did now, but he knows it wasn't good. The note should please her, anyway. He pushes himself up from the wheelchair, leans across the sink to attach the note to Maude's side of the mirror. The note falls immediately, and Dixon watches it join a graveyard of paper butterflies down by the faucet, a dozen yellow wings tattooed with the same three-word message, I'M SORRY MAUDE, I'M SORRY MAUDE, I'M SORRY MAUDE.

* * *

The kids are back. They're laying ropes of silver garland around the scarecrows.

The scarecrows were there when Dixon and Maude first moved into the house in 1967. That's something he remembers. Molly was eight, B was five. Maude didn't like them. She told Dixon to get rid of them after they moved in. They don't even look like real scarecrows, she said. That was true. They were made of wood, hand-carved, with featureless round heads atop stick figure torsos. The arms and legs were strangely bent, all wild acute angles, hieroglyphics come to life. They'll scare the children, said Maude. But Molly and B were thrilled.

Anton and Angelina. Those were their names. Of course Dixon remembers this. He even remembers the histories the kids constructed for them. He remembers that Anton was the smaller and younger of the two, reserved but fierce-hearted, a warrior—

("But he has turned away from the ways of the blade," the two agreed, speaking quietly to each other over breakfast, and the phrase *turned away from the ways of the blade* knocked on the door of Dixon's soul and slipped inside.)

—who feared lizards and cicadas, and wasn't fond of clear skies, but oh how he loved windy nights—

("Anton will be happy," one whispered from the backseat as they drove home under swaying elms from Maude's sister's place in Syracuse. And then the other: "I'm glad, after the lizard thing yesterday.")

Angelina was tall and limber and spoke four languages acquired during her years as a traveling ballerina. Born on the moon—

("The moon?" Dixon asked, skeptical. They said, "Why not the moon?")

—she had jumped too high one day during practice—

("A *grand jeté*," Mol explained.)

—and just like that, she was flung from the moon to the Earth. She wandered and danced and learned the ways of human beings—

("Human *beans*?" Dixon, horrified. "Just *stop*," they said.)

She kept her homesickness to herself. Mostly. But the moon, sometimes, made her howl. Not the full moon but the new moon, invisible in the evening sky. Angelina's moon, the kids called it, when the skies were full dark.

Maude wanted the scarecrows taken out when B died. She said they'd done no good. They'd protected no one. Dixon and Molly fought to keep them.

Dixon scrambles to withdraw the pad from his pocket. But he doesn't even know what he's trying to remember, what's worth saving about this memory. In the end he only writes MAUDE IS A TOUGH BIRD, which isn't right at all.

She has been angry, though. He knows it. Not for any specific thing Dixon has done, or if there's a specific reason then Dixon has forgotten. She's become a slammer of things. Dresser drawers, kitchen cabinets, the washing machine lid. And she swears. Good God, she swears. When she thinks he's not listening—his hearing is fine, though—she swears like a pirate under her breath. Did she always swear? He can't remember. Now everything is fuck this and motherfucker that.

A week ago he found her journal. Shouldn't have looked, he knew that. But it was a journal he'd given her a long time ago, brown leather with a gold Eiffel Tower on the cover, and as he took it in his hands he was just so happy to remember it, to remember anything, that he opened it and flipped through the pages.

The entries were few, with years between entries. Maude wasn't one to journal.

From June, 1993: *It rained all day today. I called Mol and complained too much. She said I needed a hobby and I said maybe I'd keep a diary. Dixon gave me this one so I'm going to start.*

From "The Fall, 1998": *There was a robin out in the garden that was so fat I thought it had to be my dad. Because he liked robins and he was fat himself, at least when he was in his 50s. We called him the Buddha. Well, Scotty called him that, and I laughed, but I never said it to his face.*

From January 21, 2004: *Mol came to visit. She says she's fine. We all stayed up so late talking. Dixon made us laugh. You don't think that about Dixon. You don't think he's funny but he can be.*

Then a long series of blank pages, before suddenly the entries picked up again. Only they weren't entries, just numbers that made no sense to Dixon. Like she was using the journal as a scratch pad.

0–37—320!!!
≤ 3–*25ng!*
6 × 1,200 = $7,200
12 × 1,200 = $14,400!

Then, hidden away almost at the very back of the journal, there was one last entry, undated. *Last night I dreamed he was already gone and I was glad.*

Poor damn Maude.

Dixon doesn't blame her. He knows it's a thankless job to care for him. Even though he thanks her whenever he can, often with Post-it notes.

THANKS, MAUDE, when she helps him into his clothes.

THANKS, MAUDE, when she changes his pull-up.

THANKS, MAUDE, when she bathes him, and brushes what's left of his hair, and cooks for him, and reads to him, and helps him brush his teeth, and shaves him, and scratches his back, and massages his vein-streaked legs, and takes notes at the doctor's office, and cuts his pills, and separates his pills into little compartments marked AM and PM, and helps him into bed, and whispers him back to sleep when he wakes up, lost, in the hollows of the night.

He's thought about dying. He knows he's close. Even when he's fine, when the hip doesn't hurt and his heart isn't racing and he can think clearly, the pressure in his chest is there. It isn't death. It's life squeezing him out. It's there on all sides of him, closing in, powerful and relentless, sensing the ending that's approaching and rushing to fill the vacuum.

Out in the yard, B is perched atop a thick, winding oak branch that hangs over the garden. Molly is doing snow angels down below.

Dixon is okay with the ending. With the idea of it. Well. He's almost okay. He's afraid. He shouldn't be, at his age, but he is. But it beats the alternative. It beats Maude starting to hate him. Or worse, hating herself for hating him.

A handful of pills would do the trick, he thinks. Quick and painless and no one would suspect a thing. There certainly would be no autopsy on Dixon. So the last few days, he's saved every other dose, depositing them in the sandwich bag he keeps in the pocket of his robe.

He'd like to leave Maude a note. Just to explain. To say, if he can keep the words in his head long enough to say them, what he's doing, and why. Or just to say goodbye. But what if someone else finds the note? Everyone will think he killed himself. Which, okay, yes, will be true. But there goes the insurance. Or—good God—what if they think Maude *planted* the note? What if the police get suspicious and start asking Maude questions, start wondering if she murdered him for the insurance money and used the note as an alibi?

He could tell her to destroy the note. *P.S. Maude, burn this before police arrive. Love Dixon.* Then what? The police walk in, and Maude's standing over a sink full of ashes. Looking guilty as hell. Who stands over a sink full of ashes? Murderers. Probably she'd have to make a run for it at that point. Maude! On the run! Cursing his name as she hid under a bridge somewhere, hunted down like an animal. Living off the garbage thrown from the highway above. Just lovely. A fine way to end things.

No note, then. Maude can't end up under a bridge eating garbage. Better to just let her believe he had a heart attack. Better to just let her move on.

Still.

It would be nice to at least remember the boy's name before he goes. That would be something.

Here's what Dixon can remember: The way his hair fell over his eyes no matter how he and Maude combed it, like he was a sheepdog. The way his ribs stuck out of his stomach. The way he held his breath when Dixon kissed him goodnight. The way he liked to climb, fearlessly, like a monkey. The way he smelled like rain and salt air and woodsmoke, even after a long summer's day far from the sea.

Though sunlight fills the sky, flurries are coming down. B, hanging from the branch now, swings back and forth as he prepares for his dismount.

Dixon closes his eyes. Reaches again for the boy's name. Not Bing or Benny or Basil or Bobbie or—

He fumbles for the pad, heart racing.

Not a B, but a *bie*.

This time he won't forget. This time he'll set it down. He'll have his boy back. He writes the name and underlines it, then adds six exclamation points. He just has to find a place to keep it. Someplace Maude won't find it and get upset. The sideboard! They haven't used the sideboard in fifteen years. And it's right by the window where he sits. He wheels himself over and flings opens the top-right drawer, which is filled with yellow Post-it notes, and the notes scream out at him ROB-BIE!!!! IT'S ROBBIE THE BOY'S NAME IS ROBBIE DON'T FORGET ROBBIE! NOT A B BUT A BIE ROBBIE IT'S ROBBIE! REMEMBER ROBBIE YOUR SON WAS ROBBIE THE BOY THE BOY THE BOY IS ROBBIE IT WAS MOLLY AND ROBBIE DON'T FORGET PLEASE

Fierce Pretty Things

ROBBIE HE'S WAITING FOR YOU TO REMEMBER ROBBIE YOUR BOY WAS ROBBIE HOLD ON TO ROBBIE——

Dixon's face sags. His mouth falls open. He runs his hands across the notes, and as he does so he feels the air around him closing in, squeezing him.

He looks out the window. The boy—Robbie—is no longer hanging from the oak limb. He's nowhere to be seen. Down in the snowy garden, Molly is kneeling between Anton and Angelina. The flurries are coming down harder though the sun still shines, and the wind has picked up. Molly waves frantically at Dixon, beckoning him.

"Maude," he says, his voice suddenly hoarse. Then louder, "Maude!"

Nothing. Maybe she's gone. Had she gone out somewhere without telling him?

"Robbie's hurt," he yells out. "Maude! The boy!"

Molly's hair blows in the white wind. Her face stricken.

"Maude!" he roars.

He wheels himself to the sliding glass doors that lead to the backyard. It's forty feet from the door to the garden. He can walk that far. Even in the snow, he can do it.

Gripping the door handle, he pulls himself up from the chair. The hip complains but Dixon ignores it. He hears or feels the quietest of pops inside his chest. Pressure releasing. He can breathe again. With more strength than he'd anticipated, he flings wide the sliding glass door. Winter blows into the house as Dixon steps outside. Molly, in the garden, motions him forward.

Then he's moving through the snow, he doesn't even feel the cold and he's *moving*, by God, and he calls out *I'm coming right now*, and Molly mouths the words *Hurry, hurry*, and he's trying to hurry, and then he doesn't even trip over anything, his legs simply give out beneath him and he goes down, arms flailing. He lays face down in the snow, stunned, and then he tries to get up but he can't because he can't feel his legs. Or anything below his waist. He wipes the snow from his face and pushes himself up onto his elbows. It's hard to see because of the flurries. He isn't sure where he is, where the kids are. Then he makes out Anton and Angelina. Rising up as tall as gods, clothed in silver garland. No more than twenty feet away. Dixon can go another twenty feet. By God he can at least do that. He keeps his eyes fixed on the scarecrows and begins to crawl.

Maude pulls into the garage, meanwhile, and shuts off the ignition. The car makes a series of little clicks and sighs as it falls asleep. Then it's quiet. She stares straight ahead at the back wall of the garage, gray-lit by the weak afternoon light coming through the garage door window.

God's balls, she thinks.

Dixon's tools hang neatly on a rack above a small wooden table. His chisels, his claw hammer, his brushes, his saw blades dark with rust. Along the wall beside the table is a half-finished rocking chair, a trio of bent snow shovels, shelves of old paint canisters and grout, a spinning mirror that had once stood in Molly's bedroom. The ghost of an enormous painted sunflower rises up behind it all. Its curved green stalk winds from the floor to the ceiling, then droops down, ending in a flower with a wide, toothy smile and laugh-wrinkled eyes.

Not what we desired.

That's what the doctor had said, looking down at her latest labs. There had been a discussion of options, the same discussion they'd had a month before, the same discussion—more or less—that she and Dixon had listened to when Molly became sick. She'd imagined Molly there with her in the doctor's office today, helping her ask the questions she needed to ask. She'd thought of going home to explain all this to Dixon.

Dixon.

God's balls.

For the past month she's taken up swearing as a hobby. She'd never been a swearer. It was fun at first, all those fucks and goddamns and motherfucking twats, whatever she could find on Google. The combinations were good too. *Cocksmacking motherfucking monkey fuck! Dipshit fuckwad twat goblin!* Delightful. Cathartic. Except the words lost their magic after a while, became only words again. Only *God's balls*, her own invention, had stayed in regular rotation.

She eyes the sunflower. For luck, for good fortune. That's what Molly told them, when they caught her with the paint brush. After forty years, maybe it needed another coat.

It isn't that she's dying. Or that Dixon is dying. It's only that she'll get weak. It's only that she will, very possibly, die before him and leave him alone to face what's coming, without understanding a damn thing that's happening. She'll have to find a place for him, and find the money to pay for it, and arrange to sell the house, and keep all of this a secret from Dixon. Who won't know what's going on but will feel the weight of it and will know that she's the one bearing the weight.

She has wished—has caught herself wishing—that he was gone. That she'll walk in the room and he's passed quietly away in his chair. Wouldn't it be better? How could it not be better than what's to come? She's even thought about doing it herself. It wouldn't take much—a handful of Demerol would do the job. God knows Dixon has asked for it. He has pleaded with her, though he never remembers. Which kills her.

But she can't. She can't do it, among other reasons, because of the string of Post-it notes in her glove compartment, which Dixon wrote, stapled together, and left on her bedside table last Monday.

MAUDE I KNOW THINGS HAVEN'T BEEN GOOD AND I'M SORRY BUT I WANT YOU TO KNOW I'VE BEEN HAPPY ALL THIS TIME ALL MY LIFE AND THANK YOU FOR THAT AND IF IN THE NEXT LIFE YOU WANT TO BE WITH ME WHEREVER THAT IS THEN I WOULD LIKE THAT TOO MAUDE. AND IF NOT THEN I'M STILL HAPPY I GOT THIS. IT WAS AN HONOR TO KNOW YOU. DIXON.

So, no. There's no way she's murdering Dixon. Not when he is who he is, and who he always was. He writes this to her and she's going to euthanize him? God's balls.

She actually did try to tell him the truth. He was lucid then too. I get it, Maude, he said. Grim but reassuring. We'll figure this out. And he patted her hand. *He* patted *her* hand. And in that moment, dear God, she believed him. There was still enough left of the old Dixon, the one who fixed things, that she believed him. Then an hour later he was back at the window, the matter forgotten, looking out at his goddamn scarecrows.

What sad, strange things. She understands why he kept them. Well, no, she understands that they meant something to Dixon, even if he never spoke of it. Of the boy. Always too much for him. *On my watch.* That's what he said, over and over, at the hospital that day. But it was an accident. A fall on the playground, of all things. Blamed himself. Of course he blamed himself. Maybe she did, too, for a while. But Dixon was blameless.

Not what we desired. That's all it was.

And she doesn't blame him now for trying to remember. For asking, again and again, about *the boy.* About Molly. It's only that she's tired, and, well, they were supposed to figure everything out together.

Her shoulders fall, though she isn't aware she's been holding them up all this time. A trick of the light as the shadows creep up the garage wall: the sunflower dips its massive head lower, a giant peering in through the windshield at her.

She thinks, Maybe it's time.

Maybe it's time for both of them. While Dixon still recognizes her. Before he has to watch her slow fade from his life, without ever understanding or remembering why.

They'll sit together. Yes, yes. She'll wait until he's feeling good. Before the sun goes down, when the light is forgiving and she can see in his eyes that he's seeing a younger, warmer, more open-hearted version of herself. A version of herself that she doesn't always believe in any longer.

Is it now?

The sunflower fades, disappears into the gray evening.

It's quiet in the garage. Everything is still. Her heart, even her heart is still. She thinks, It must be now. That must be why my heart is still. She looks around the garage one last time, takes the keys out of the ignition, and goes inside.

She feels the cold air, hears the wind before she even sees the open sliding glass door. Dixon's wheelchair, empty. She goes to the door, and her heart is no longer still, and she looks out and sees him in the garden, down on the ground in the snow, wearing only his robe. His arms and his body are wrapped tightly around the smaller scarecrow's legs. His

Fierce Pretty Things

silver hair flies madly in the snow. Maude drops her purse and rushes to him, snow in her eyes, and she thinks, Not yet, not yet, oh Christ not yet. Dixon lifts his head and sees her. His face is shining, triumphant. He says, I've got him, I've got him, Maude, and he extends one arm and reaches for her to pull her close, to bring them together, to bring them all together and keep them safe.

6

Grandfather Vampire

The nickname came from Praeger, of course, who said it was because Mr. Leary looked like a vampire who'd stepped into the sunlight a million years ago and got bleached white as bone, and was condemned to walk the earth in torment, only he ended up in Westover married to Mrs. Leary, who taught us grammar. The name stuck, but kids mostly didn't like Grandfather Vampire on account of the story Eddie Pastornicky told in second grade about seeing him fire a salt pellet at Rusty, who was Eddie Pastornicky's neighbor's Lhasa Apso, but there was also speculation that he was just mean because of some spell of tragedy way back. Maybe from the war, but we didn't know which war, since we didn't know exactly how old he was (between forty and eighty-five was the speculation), or when the wars in question had actually happened.

And anyway, Mrs. Leary never said anything about a tragedy. When she talked about Grandfather Vampire it was to instruct us on not making damn fool decisions, like for example Mr. Leary wanting to buy the Super 130 drive-in movie theater that was buried in the high weeds behind the Shute Beach apartments, despite Mr. Leary not knowing anything, as Mrs. Leary put it, about anything. She liked to teach us moral lessons along with the grammar.

Mrs. Leary died the third week of June right after school let out, and for the next two weeks nobody saw Mr. Leary out on his porch. The lawn got overgrown pretty quick and the lights were always off, and there was some speculation that he was dead, too, probably because of some damn fool thing he'd done, only we were all too scared to knock on the door to check on account of Rusty the Lhasa Apso, and also him being Grandfather Vampire.

Then one night when it was still early in the summer I was staying over at Praeger's, in the back bedroom of one of the second-story units at Shute Beach, and Praeger turned out the lights so we could discuss the five most terrifying nightmares we ever had, and he looked out his window and said, "Son of a bitch," which is what he always says. I got up and looked and I saw it too: a light burning in the projectionist's booth at the Super 130, and a long thin shadow bent nearly in half, the head bobbing up and down now and then. Praeger grabbed his binoculars and said, "Son of a bitch," then handed them to me and I said, "Son of a bitch." Because it was Grandfather Vampire who was standing there in that booth, holding a screwdriver as if he'd never seen one before in his life. Praeger grabbed the binoculars back from me, then I grabbed them back from him, and it went on like that for a while, neither of us saying a damn thing. Then the light went out in the projectionist's booth and we saw Mr. Leary drive away. Praeger said, "I'm gonna go fix it for him," and then he was hanging out the window by his fingertips and then he jumped, without even bothering to put on his shoes, exactly like a damn fool. But I followed him.

Took him the better part of the night to fix the projector, and took me running back and forth to get supplies all night, and in between there was a lot of Praeger scowling and asking where the hell the intermittent sprocket was, and who the hell designed these cambers, et cetera, which I figured was mostly an excuse for him to say *hell* and to show off, but he got it fixed. He wrote up some notes for Mr. Leary on how to thread the reels, then we left.

Next night I was back at Praeger's and we watched through the binoculars as Mr. Leary came back to the booth. He saw what Praeger had done, read the note. Looked out the window. Left the booth. Praeger and me started discussing top five most lethal creatures on the planet not including snakes. Hour later Mr. Leary came back carrying two reels of film. Hour after that he was still sitting on the floor of the booth, film everywhere, looking damn lost, looking exactly like an old lost vampire.

Praeger sighed and said "Son of a bitch," and started getting dressed.

Short time later I was leaning against the inside of the booth while Praeger got the reels threaded up. Mr. Leary stood off to the side watching him work, bony arms hugging his shoulders, and every few seconds he looked over my way. I was doing my best to become invisible, on account of suddenly remembering the time a few years back when Grandfather Vampire almost backed over me with his car as I was riding my Big Wheel past his house. Dragged me home and stood there in the doorway with one bony hand clutching my shoulder as he yelled at my mom. But he didn't let on if he remembered now. Just nodded at me when he finally caught my eye, and I nodded back.

Praeger finally got it all set up, and a minute later we were sitting out front of the booth in lawn chairs, amidst the high weeds, watching Mr. Leary's movie. Only it wasn't a movie exactly, just a white screen. Or almost a white screen, because you could see some shadows moving around and whatnot, but that was about it. ("Son of a bitch," I whispered to Praeger, but he just ignored me and kept watching.)

Mr. Leary stayed in the booth and didn't say a thing during the film. But when it was over he offered us both a dollar a night to come out the rest of the summer, every night around midnight, till school started up again. Praeger to run the projector and me to do concessions, which seemed like the easier job to me on account of there not being any actual customers per se.

So the next night we snuck out again, and Praeger found a new set of reels waiting for him and got them threaded up while I pretended to do stuff around the concession stand. Once the movie started we watched from the lawn chairs, eating stale popcorn and drinking some questionable root beer that Praeger'd brought from his basement. Mr. Leary, same as before, watched from the booth. Hands folded in his lap, body like a stone, only his eyes completely alive as he watched the screen.

Still wasn't what I'd call a movie. No title at all, just started straight off with what looked like a funeral. ("In media res," Praeger said, and I said, "Yeah sure." Damn Praeger.) Only a handful of people at the gravesite, which seemed sad enough to me, but the scene was notable mainly because of the damn small casket they were lowering into the ground. Reminded me a lot of Donnie. Not his actual funeral, but I mean the way everything looked that day. Sun was going down in the background and it was mad beautiful, all violets and golds like something out of a dream. I'd wanted to say something at the time but didn't, since nobody wants to hear about some beautiful sky at a funeral. I wouldn't want to hear that either. So I apologized to Donnie in my head and kept my mouth shut.

People finally started to leave. It was autumn and bronze leaves were falling and again I thought it was kind of a pretty scene, spite of everything. Then the camera just hung around the grave for a little too long, which didn't please me any. I started to itch. Looked over at Praeger and he refused to even raise his eyebrows like he does sometimes to make me feel less nervous.

Then, son of a bitch, a hand came snaking out of that grave. I bounced off the lawn chair and took off running, but when I looked back Praeger hadn't moved, barely even looked in my direction. I had a mind to head straight back to Shute Beach and crawl in the window, only I didn't on account of not wanting to be in Praeger's bedroom by myself. Instead I hung out at the edge of the lot with my back up against the fence so as to not expose myself to a surprise attack.

A few minutes later Praeger ambled over, now with his eyebrows raised.

"You know I got a thing with zombies," I said. Embarrassed a little but not much, since it was Praeger.

"Ain't zombies," he said. "Just come on back."

"Call me when the zombies are gone," I said.

"Can't," he said, sounding exasperated, "since the damn movie stopped when you ran off."

"Son of a bitch," I said, and Praeger agreed. So I went back with him, and he was right. That hand was still frozen on the screen, just coming out of the ground, only now the image was flickering a little as if the projector lamp was dying.

"Looks busted," I said, but Praeger just shook his head and sat down, so I sat down too.

And the movie started back up right away.

Maybe Praeger didn't think it was a zombie movie, but I don't know what else but a zombie crawls out of a grave like that. Just a kid, younger than me and Praeger even, but still a zombie. Mouth hanging open and face covered in mud, hair matted down with mud, mud in his eyes. Dressed all in a nice suit, though, which I figured made sense, and I wondered why more movie zombies didn't go around in nice clothes. One of his nice shoes had come off.

My stomach was flopping some but I kept watching. You could see it was a struggle for him to walk, plus his mouth kept falling open and flies were buzzing all around him like he was a hamburger that got dropped on the side of the road. He must've walked a couple of miles, dragging his left leg behind him like a prisoner with one of those balls attached to his leg. Trying to breathe, which didn't make any sense to me, but I thought maybe he just remembered what breathing was like and thought he was *supposed* to breathe. Anyway, the sound gave me the jeebs.

The town he was walking through started looking familiar. Not exactly the same—like, for instance, Pemby's Auto Parts on Washington was called Pendee's Auto Parts in the movie. But familiar even so. And then the middle school. The cut-through on Henderson. When he walked past Spider Park I turned to Praeger and started to say son of a bitch, but Praeger shushed me and said just keep watching.

He finally made it home, then just stood there in front of the door with the flies buzzing around him, caked in mud, wearing that one shoe, mouth hanging open. Rang the doorbell. Footsteps coming, and I knew who'd be on the other side. She'd scream when she saw her son standing there, and after she screamed she'd collapse on the floor. Then he'd eat her brains without a doubt. I decided I wasn't going to watch that part, no matter what Praeger said.

Instead the dad opened the door. Tall, thin, with hollowed-out eyes, but a young face, younger and kinder than I expected. He kneeled down slow, the way you would with a dog you aren't quite sure is friendly. And then the zombie boy just sort of lurched forward and fell into his arms. And now the brain eating had to begin, anybody could see that. But the dad only hugged him close, exposing his vulnerable skull, and the boy hung there in his dad's arms, still trying to breathe, rattling his dead lungs. I realized I was holding my breath.

And then, real slow, the zombie boy began to crumble away. Like sand running out through a busted hourglass. His dad was left kneeling on the floor with his arms wrapped around a pile of clothes and mud. And the screen went white.

For a few seconds Praeger and me didn't move. I looked over and he gave me the eyebrows, and I gave him the eyebrows back.

When we got up, Mr. Leary wasn't in the booth. Praeger shut off the lights and the projector. We walked back to his place and I didn't say a word, since I could tell Praeger was thinking.

"Gonna need a staple gun," he said after a while, and I said, "Of course."

Next day we sat down in Praeger's basement and made up a hundred flyers. Secret midnight showing at Grandfather Vampire's Super 130. Below that was a title: "Zombie Boy Returns." Praeger had me draw a little zombie doodle beneath the title on each of the flyers, and by the time we were done I was swearing like mad and couldn't hardly move my hand anymore. We walked outside and the sun hurt our eyes from being tucked away in the basement. In two hours we had the flyers stapled from one end of Westover to the other, and by then it would've been harder to miss those flyers than to find one of them.

Still, only Gus Hargrove and Eddie Pastornicky showed up the first night. Dragged their sleeping bags in through the busted gate and I nodded and handed them bags of stale popcorn while Praeger got things started inside.

Gus looked up at the screen. "What is it," he said.

"Are you gonna ask questions the whole time?" I said. "Damn."

He shrugged.

The movie started up. Praeger and me took our regular positions, and Gus and Eddie found a spot clear of the high weeds and settled in.

Zombie boy came back to life in his dad's arms, reappearing out of the sad little pile of mud and graveclothes right there in the foyer. Which was a nice way to start. I eyed Gus and Eddie to make sure they appreciated it.

His name was Emilio, turned out. Not exactly a classic monster name, in my opinion, although Emilio was looking less like a monster tonight anyways. His dad got him cleaned up and dressed in some regular, non-grave clothes, brushed his hair, and made sure he was presentable for his mom. Then they sat together in the kitchen and waited. Mom finally walked in carrying a vase of flowers, noticed the muddy footsteps, and followed the trail to the kitchen. Took one look at zombie boy—at Emilio—and again I was sure she would scream, or at least drop those flowers and the vase would shatter. But she just came to the table and sat down with Emilio and his dad. Put her hand on Emilio's head, Emilio kind of half-smiling on account of not being able to use his face completely just yet, on account of still being halfway dead. And she looked back at the dad and nodded. Like, okay, sure, we're doing this thing with Emilio coming back from the dead and whatnot.

They had to teach him pretty much everything all over again. How to walk regular without shuffling like a monster. How to brush his teeth and dress himself. How to talk, which was something that he never seemed to really get a hang of, or maybe he was just always a little quiet, even before being a zombie. I thought that was possible. Donnie was quiet and took a long time to answer questions sometimes, but I never thought it was because he was slow. Just liked to think about things first, was all.

The movie ended with Emilio's first day back to school. Nervous, holding his backpack, same backpack I had last year with a robot dinosaur on it. Trying not to let his mouth hang open in that zombie way he had. Stepped into the school and kids started looking around, and you could tell things were going to get bad in a hurry. We read *Frankenstein* last year in Mrs. Leary's class, so I knew everyone was going to turn on Emilio pretty quick now, and then I had to think he would be forced to eat their brains. Only maybe we wouldn't mind so much, watching, since we knew he just wanted to fit in, same as Frankenstein's monster, and why couldn't they just let him alone already.

Only once again things didn't go that way. Kids just came over to Emilio and smiled at him, and shook his hand, and touched his clothes, and tousled his hair. And Emilio smiled back, at least the left half of his mouth did. Tried to say something that came out in a grave-y kind of way, and nobody screamed. One of the teachers came out to see him and took him by the hand and walked him to class. The sun was coming in through the windows, and it was that same crazy sky out there, and the light shining on Emilio made him look kind of nice, even sitting there with his mouth hanging open a bit. And that's how the movie ended.

By the next night we had a dozen more kids, and Praeger and me had to clear out some of the weeds to make room.

Emilio was back on the playground with the other kids. Building a go-kart with his dad. Having dinner with his parents. Reading books. Still didn't say a whole lot, like Donnie, and sometimes when he was thinking about something real hard, or when he was alone, he could look kind of sad, kind of lost. Sometimes he opened his closet door and saw his old graveclothes hanging up in there, all cleaned up now. Didn't say anything, just looked at them.

But when he smiled, I swear there was something a little beautiful about him. Almost glowed sometimes, even, when he was happy. When does somebody glow like that? A few times I caught myself leaning forward, smiling, when some other kid would pick up one of Emilio's books that had dropped out of his bag, or hold the door open for him, that kind of thing. Kids aren't always friendly like that. Good things don't always happen like that. But I wanted good things to happen for Emilio because of how he looked when he was happy. Everybody did. You could see that.

More and more kids started coming to the drive-in, sneaking out after their families had gone to bed. For some reason they stuck around and came back again the next night, and the next. Sometimes things were exciting, like the time Emilio tried to climb up the water tower and fell twenty feet and everybody thought he was dead all over again, for real this time (but he wasn't, broken leg was all, and he got to wear a bright green cast just like Gus had that time a few years back, which made Gus hoot when he saw it). But mostly things were quiet, not all that dramatic. Just a regular kind of life. But kids kept coming to the drive-in to see what would happen next. They were worried when Emilio had to get up to deliver a speech in class. They laughed when Emilio went to the beach with his mom and dad and they all built sand zombies. When Emilio came home one day with a Lhasa Apso puppy, every kid at the drive-in cheered, even Eddie Pastornicky. And every night when the movie ended, we shuffled out through the high weeds and walked like ghosts ourselves through the Westover streets back to our homes, talking a little about what we'd seen, but mostly just quiet, thinking our own private thoughts, I guess.

Westover got to be a little strange, come late July. Kids were so tired from the late nights that they slept half the day away, and when they did come outside, the sun was too bright to take. We avoided playgrounds and ball fields and instead took to gathering in basements and garages and other places that didn't get a whole lot of sun. And we'd talk about what we'd all seen the night before at Grandfather Vampire's drive-in.

There was a good deal of speculation. Older kids, the more sophisticated ones, were starting to think something bad was coming. You don't come back from the dead, reasoning went, without some repercussions. Possibilities were discussed. A fire. A car accident. Disease. Sooner or later something was going to send Emilio back to the grave.

I didn't try to guess. Maybe I just didn't care what was supposed to happen anymore. Maybe I just wanted him to grow up, like he was doing, and just be happy.

"But that ain't a movie," Praeger said, when I told him that. We were on our way to the drive-in one night in late July.

"I don't care," I said.

"Yeah," Praeger said, "I know."

July turned into August. Emilio grew up. He went to high school and tried out for the football team. Didn't make it, not having ever really mastered the hand–eye coordination thing or the running thing, but everybody liked him so much that they made him team president, which I didn't even know was a thing. He wasn't the smartest kid, or the most athletic, or the most anything, really. But he did okay. And as he got older he never got mean. He just stayed good, is I guess what I'm saying. And I was happy because not everybody stays good.

August wore on. By the middle of the month we had more than a hundred kids camped out every night. I didn't know half of them. They staggered in with their sleeping bags and their lawn chairs and sometimes their stuffed animals, too, half asleep, collecting their popcorn and finding an open space wherever they could. Grandfather Vampire sat in the booth and never spoke and was always gone by the end. Praeger and me watched from our usual spot. Sometimes I'd look over at Praeger and wonder what he was thinking, but he didn't say much.

Emilio graduated high school and joined the military. Fought in some distant place, and saw people around him die. We all had some nervous moments then, but Emilio survived. Won some medals. Came home, only not glowing so much. The town threw a party for him, same way they did with Praeger's older brother Buddy.

He went back to school, to college. Met a girl named Raisa, which was my mom's name. When they got married they bought a house at the top of Sunset Hill. Adopted a Lhasa Apso and named him Rusty.

And they had a baby too. Most beautiful baby boy you ever saw, except that he was sick, he was born sick. And everyone knew this was coming, that sooner or later something awful had to happen, and kids were looking at each other and shaking their heads.

Baby's name was Donnie.

It was the last week of the summer. Storms were coming in but the rains held up while we watched Emilio and Raisa talk to the doctor, while we saw Donnie get a little older, just old enough to start to be a real kid, with an imagination, just starting to figure out who he was going to be. We saw the months slip away. Saw Donnie going in for an operation. Saw Emilio leave the hospital one night and walk back through the town toward the cemetery, the cemetery he'd once been buried in, and kneel down there, with the sun dying behind him. His father was there, too, old Grandfather Vampire himself, reaching his old bony hand down to grasp Emilio's shoulder, squeezing it tight.

I got up and walked to the booth, which I knew would be empty. Just stood there, the movie playing behind me.

"Going home," I said to Praeger, and then I left.

* * *

Next night around eleven-thirty, Praeger came by my house and threw something at the window. When I didn't answer he threw something bigger. I said son of a bitch to myself and threw open the window. "I ain't going," I called down. Then I went back to bed.

Some noisy minutes later, Praeger hauled himself over the windowsill.

"What the hell," he said, seeing me under the covers.

"Told you I ain't going," I said. "I'm tired, Praeger."

"I need you," he said. "To do the concessions and whatnot."

I rolled over so my back was to him, fairly miserable, and said, "I'm going to sleep."

"It's the finale," he said. "We gotta see what happens. To Emilio. To everybody. All this time? We gotta see."

I didn't say anything.

"So you're going to be a coward, is that it?" he demanded.

Damn Praeger. I sat up and turned to face him. "Everybody dies. There. I just told you the end, you dumbass. Now get out of here."

"How do you know?"

I didn't say anything, just squeezed my eyes shut. When Praeger asked again, I said, "He took everything else. He can't have Donnie."

Praeger didn't have an answer for that. So he just said, real quiet, "But you don't know. What's going to happen, I mean. You don't really know."

Fierce Pretty Things

"Seen this movie before," I said. And I dropped back down and turned away.

Next thing I knew, Praeger's hands were underneath me and he was lifting me up out of bed. "You're going to see the goddamn finale," he said.

I didn't fight him. I outweigh Praeger by a few pounds, so I was curious to see how far he'd get with me. He made it two steps toward the window. Then we went down in a heap, Praeger landing underneath me. Knocked the wind out of both of us.

I rolled off him. After we both caught our breath, I said, "What were you going to do when you got to the damn window?"

He shrugged. "Hadn't thought that far ahead," he said.

I sighed and said, "Okay, fine. Let's just go see the damn finale."

* * *

The rains were coming, the end of summer rains that always came to Westover. It was a warm night and the stars were gone and the summer was gone, too, but the rains were coming.

The lot at the Super 130 was empty. I looked at Praeger and he shrugged. "So it'll just be us," he said.

I walked into the projectionist's booth with him. Grandfather Vampire wasn't there either, but there was one last reel on the chair where he always sat.

"I'll get it set up quick," Praeger said. "Before the rains come. You go out and sit down."

"Doesn't feel right," I said.

"Go sit down," said Praeger.

I walked out of the booth and sat down. Looked around at the lot for the first time in quite a while. The asphalt had cracked open in a hundred places. Weeds had taken over so much that you could barely see the screen anymore without standing up. Looked as much like a cemetery, that moment, as any place I'd ever been.

The movie started up.

It was different now. Just like a regular home movie, the kind your dad makes with one of those old video recorders. All different scenes of birthdays and band recitals and soccer games and family vacations, all running together one after the other, as if that's all life was, just high-lights, one happy celebration after another. Only in these home movies it was Donnie, and it was me, and we were the ones having birthdays, and playing games whenever Donnie wasn't feeling so bad, and going on vacation when Donnie could take some time away from the hospi-tal. Here was Donnie and me running through the sprinklers in the backyard. Here was Donnie holding my hand on his first day of kinder-garten, when I kept trying to shrug him off but he wouldn't let go and finally I told myself to hell with it and just let him keep holding it. Here was Donnie holding up a present I'd given him for his seventh birthday, some stupid book I found and I thought he'd love because it was about the pyramids and he was just a nutjob about the pyramids for a while. Here was the hospital bed, that stupid damn hospital bed. Here was my brother Donnie. Just waving at the camera and smiling. And I thought, just stop waving, what the hell are you waving for, and there's me, refus-ing to get in the car, refusing to say goodbye because it's a stupid god-damn thing to say. And then it was over, and the movie ran out, and all that was left was the sound of the reel flapping in the projector, and the wind coming down to sweep through the parking lot before the rains.

I walked back to the booth. Praeger was gone. I found the switch for the projector and turned it off, not bothering to take off the last reel. Looked around one last time, then shut off the lights.

When I walked out I figured it would be too dark to see, but there was some moonlight coming in through the clouds. I thought maybe I would see him. Even though the movie was over, I thought just maybe I would see him.

But the screen was dark. It shimmered like a curtain in the wind. And I just stood and watched it through the high weeds, in the last sec-onds of the summer, before the rains came.

7

The Magnificents

Woke up around midnight to explosions and helicopters. Must have dozed off on sofa due to long day, also being drunk. Looked around for Bo, expecting worst because of the fireworks, found he'd already eaten all the padding in his crate. Fortunately able to get him outside before it came out other end. Poor dog, terrible nerves.

Got dressed and grabbed bottle from wine fridge as party gift, set out into steamy June night. Stinton's place lit up like a Christmas tree. Guy dressed as the Reaper getting bludgeoned by dwarves on small stage on front lawn. Impressive number of dwarves, couldn't have been cheap. Only a few spectators, including Margot's old kindergarten teacher, Nora Quincy. Nora Quincy dressed in familiar FUCK DEATH IN THE ASS T-shirt, the one that showed Death bent over a coffin, being fucked in the ass, eyeballs crossed due to pain and terrible humiliation, et cetera. I waved but she didn't notice me, too happy/enraged by show.

Realized as I got to the door that I'd brought wrong bottle. Brought bottle from private stash, left over from winemaking days. Meat-flavored. Many arguments with Gwen regarding idea; Gwen correct. Smashed bottle against side of house just as Bonnie answered the door. Meat smells drifted up, also notes of citrus and blackberry. Tried to explain to Bonnie about the smell. She frowned and asked if I was armed and I said ha ha, no.

Lively party. Chocolate fondue fountain, fire-eating demonstration, live Sumatran tiger. Also dead, stuffed Sumatran tiger. Lots of toasts to Stinton, and the usual chorus of people chanting. "A hundred more, a hundred more." Plus some speeches outlining contributions to society, exemplary Net Social Value, great work ethic, et cetera. Then a poem in Stinton's honor, recited by granddaughter, current Poet Laureate of United States. Humbling.

Talked with Stinton a little. Hadn't talked much since the thing with Cleo. Who, speaking of, was running around at party and looked totally fine, I thought. Very slight limp due to missing leg but otherwise fine. Labradoodles more resilient than friendships, maybe. Friendships more easily mangled under wheels of fate/hybrid vehicle, leaving guts splattered everywhere. Metaphorically, not real friendship guts.

Told Stinton that Cleo looked good. Told him he, Stinton, didn't look a hundred, didn't even look sixty. Which was true. Looked waxy, but not old. Young and waxy. Then was asked by Dr. Wilhelm to keep reasonable distance from Stinton during conversation and to point face in other direction. So had to speak at weirdly high volume. Didn't take offense. Wilhelm could be my Personal Aging Physician someday, if lucky. Would want him to protect me from unnecessary risks, to tell suspicious-looking neighbor without invitation to point face in other direction.

A good talk anyway. Bonded with Stinton some. Felt better about things, friendshipwise. Screamed at wall, Glad we had this time to catch up! Then wandered around, drank some. Not too much. Didn't want to look like clod at Stinton's party.

Fierce Pretty Things

Ran into Gwen and her lover. Helena, or maybe Elaine. Gwen said nice to see me again. I gulped more champagne, also double tequila shot. Kind of a sad thing to say. Nice to see me again. Like we were old high school friends maybe. Or like she was popular girl in high school and vaguely remembered me as kid with weird teeth (now fixed!). Like we hadn't spent ten years together, didn't have two grown kids. Like I'd never made her laugh with my pretend Italian, or surprised her on thirtieth birthday with brochure for Venice trip we never took. Like she'd forgotten I used trip money to send away for gelato franchise quickstart book/DVD series.

She asked what I was doing now. Told her I was basically managing things at the office. Not sure why I said that. Dumb thing to say, began to sweat. Explained imaginary new management responsibilities in detail. Took another tequila shot. Felt shaky, pictured conversation in mind as train speeding toward collapsing bridge. She said she was just promoted to vice president of North American sales at Pfizer, and I said wow. Pretended I hadn't read her feature profile in weekend *Magazine* section. Downed another shot, imagined conversation plunging off bridge, screaming passengers, monkeys. Not sure why monkeys. Learned she was in town promoting first book, *Follow Through*. She gave me a complimentary copy. Signed and addressed it to me using both our full names. I said well it was nice to see her, then threw up on Elaine's/Helena's boobs.

Left shortly thereafter. Saw guy who played Reaper walking to his car. Nice guy. Some broken ribs but he said the gig paid well, couldn't complain.

Went home and sat in backyard with Bo and had nightcap. Threw up. Think Bo ate it, not sure.

* * *

Called in sick next morning.

I thought you were fired in the last round of layoffs, Toby said.

I asked if Meg was in today. Meg worked in reception, very pretty despite cloudy eye from glaucoma. Maybe prettier because of cloudy eye somehow?

She's right here, Toby said. Want me to put her on? He asked Meg if she wanted to talk to me, and she said why. Toby said he didn't know why, maybe I was in love with her. Then they both laughed.

Toby came back on the phone. Anyways, he said. Yeah, she's here.

I said thanks. Said I was taking off Friday, too, for fiftieth birthday.

Must be nice, he said. To be so young!

I said yes, yes. Nice to be young.

*   *   *

Sat outside on patio with Bo the rest of morning. Good to be outside in the sunshine, though Bo still having intestinal problems due to crate padding in guts, et cetera.

Stinton's party was on my mind. Maybe extravagant, sure, but symbolized life's accomplishments. Symbolized grabbing hold of life by throat, as Gwen always said. Only: never much wanted to grab hold of life by throat, strangle life until tigers, dwarves popped out. Never desired enough, Gwen said. Head stuck in the clouds. Endearing at first, then maddening for Gwen. Needed me to want more. I said, More what? Just more, she said. Otherwise would never accomplish anything! And would drag everyone else down, like obese unemployed guy in HEY PARASITE! comic strip. Obese guy always taking, even when just daydreaming and enjoying flowers at public park. Doesn't realize he's blocking view of flowers for adorable little girl sitting on lap of decorated war veteran in wheelchair, both of them holding tiny American flags. Then obese guy leaves and tosses subsidized candy wrapper on adorable little girl's head, makes her cry.

Took out notepad and started writing new resolution list.

Get in shape. Depressing, kind of. Implied existing shapelessness. Crossed out and wrote, *Continue lifelong improvement of shape.* Felt better, wrote *in progress* in margin. *Take Bo for more walks.* Which could also be part of shape-improvement plan. Felt like I was maximizing efficiencies already. *Learn French.* Italian harder than expected, maybe French easier? Imagined running into Gwen on streets of Paris. Saying nice to see you again, but with debonair French accent. Or some quote from Voltaire, et cetera. Something withering? No. Something thoughtful, kind. Then: tip beret and move quietly on, serene, dignified. *Bond more with Margot and/or Philip.* Tricky. Philip: more resentful, claims bankruptcy/divorce ruined high school experience and denied him chance at non-state-university education. Blames me for lack of direction, occasional trouble with law, having daughter with wooden arm. Margot: less resentful, friendly sometimes. But calls me Uncle Mike, tells people real dad named "Brian David Winston," killed in line of duty during shootout with serial killer. Keeps scrapbook of real dad. Weird.

Dozed off while shopping online for berets. Dreamed I was a boy again. Down in basement, preparing for first/last performance in front of Mom, Dad, Janet. Michael the Magnificent. Full of joy because in dream, could really do magic. Not just tricks. Family walked in and sat down. Smiling. Anticipating a good show. Nothing up my sleeve. You'll see Baxter is inside this simple box, et cetera. You'll see this is a normal saw taken from the shed, et cetera. Golden magician light shone down from Golden Magician! brand spotlight purchased with own money. Thought to self: this is really happy moment. At peace, confident. Unlike in real life, dream family enjoyed the show. No screaming at all. Just wonder.

Woke up to Bo slinking away from fresh pile of something in corner of living room. Poor dog.

*   *   *

Went through mail after dinner. Usual stuff. Next to last notice, et cetera. You have been preapproved. List of neighborhood Centennials. *Stop in and say hello and congratulations!*

Was hoping for maybe a birthday card from Margot. Not expecting one from Philip, but maybe from Margot. *Just between us, still think of you as real dad. Sorry re: Brian David Winston. Happy BDay. M.*

No card, though. Maybe sent it today so card would arrive on Friday? Or even later. *P.S. Sorry this is so late. Wanted to make sure found the perfect card!*

Last thing was ad from Retirement Recruiters. Congratulated me on upcoming Semicentennial, asked where I would be in fifty years. Helpful cartoon with two possible scenarios. Scenario 1: cartoon version of me dressed in tuxedo, sipping champagne on yacht, and surrounded by happy great-grandchildren. Heart bubbles floating out of heads of great-grandchildren, signifying love and appreciation. Scenario 2: cartoon version of me living in refrigerator box, hairless and ugly. Surrounded by hairless and ugly great-grandchildren in slightly smaller refrigerator boxes, with no heart bubbles. Not sure why great-grandchildren hairless in scenario 2. Familiar RR logo on the back, man in top hat dancing into coffin, children holding hands encircling globe behind him. *Take One for the Team! Early Retirement Pay-Out Option Starts at 50!*

Tossed in recycling and went for walk with Bo. Passed by Stinton and Bonnie sitting on their porch drinking mint juleps served by robot butler. Yelled howdy and Stinton kind of nodded toward Bo and me, then closed security gate. Probably Bo reminded him of Cleo, friendship guts, et cetera. Also saw Bridge Guy. Not real name, Bridge Guy. Assume not real name. Came up with name when Margot/Philip were kids, family still together. Margot: Why is bearded guy in army uniform always hanging out under bridge, carrying garbage bag? Me: Because he's Bridge Guy! Sounded better than deranged homeless veteran. Like maybe he had special powers. Philip always terrified of Bridge Guy, but Margot fascinated. Said he was noble savage. Wrote poems about Bridge Guy, drew pictures of him that she left in garbage cans for him to find. Sweet, weird. Then one day Margot announced that Bridge Guy made her feel bad and she wanted to stop believing in him.

Found him sitting on curb now. Waved at him and said, Nice sunset! But he didn't look over. Eyes blank and mouth hanging open, maybe just his sunset-enjoying face? Waved again and kept walking. Few steps later Bridge Guy stood up and staggered forward, flailing arms like zombie, or like sad homeless person. I grabbed a random bill from my wallet. Left it on sidewalk, headed quickly around corner with Bo.

Reached the field at the Civil War park and Bo sat down, wouldn't move. Maybe tired out due to infrequent walks. I said let's get back for special treats and he pretended to fall asleep, knew from past experience special treats actually green beans.

Chubby kid out in the field. Running back and forth, trying to fly kite despite windless day. Wearing a hunting cap with ear flaps, unfortunate. Also using way too much string, so kite by this point just

Fierce Pretty Things

dragging along ground, shredded to pieces. Now and then chubby kid leaped into air like superhero. Knocked down repeatedly by gravity, being chubby kid. He looked up after a while and saw us and trotted over.

Is your dog dead, he said.

He's pretending to be asleep, I told him.

He said why does he have padding coming out of his butt.

Long story, I said. Told him he needed to use less string until the kite was airborne. And a windy day would help.

He said thanks. Said he wished he was older, like me, so he'd just know things like that.

I agreed it was nice to be old.

He said his name was Kozma. It's Greek, he said.

Told him my name was Mike. He asked what kind of name Mike was, and I said it wasn't really any kind of name as far as I knew. Said I had a granddaughter with a wooden arm a few years younger than him, named Kady with a *K*.

Wooden arm, he said, but real fingers?

I said I thought she had wooden fingers, too, but couldn't say for sure because I'd never met her. Also a long story.

He took off his cap. Crazy hair flew in every direction. You like to hunt? he said.

I said not really.

He nodded and said, Me neither. His dad, the judge, was a hunter. Had tracked and caught a runner last year. Killed him with his bare hands, snapped his neck. Bounty money was going to pay for his whole college education.

I said that's impressive, and Kozma agreed.

He asked if I'd ever beaten anyone up, and I said no. He asked if I'd ever been beaten up myself.

I told him I was mugged once. Coming out of the train station with Philip, when he was nine. Pictured tiny Philip in mind's eye. So serious, holding model airplane he'd bought at gift shop back in Philadelphia.

Kozma said, Did you fight back?

I shook my head.

Because your boy was there, he said. You didn't want to risk it.

The Magnificents

I told him I was just scared. Hands were shaking when I gave thief wallet and wristwatch, birthday present from Gwen. Didn't say that thief also took Philip's model airplane. Who steals kid's airplane? Philip speechless, furious. Demanded I chase thief down, beat him senseless, set him on fire. I told him we'd let police handle it. Philip was silent for next two days, communicated only via glares. When he got back to Philadelphia, told Gwen he wanted to sign up for tae kwon do lessons.

Kozma looked at me sideways, as if he knew all of that. As if he was reevaluating me in light of this new information.

Well, he said. Good luck with your dog.

*   *   *

Birthday started out okay. Quiet, just Bo and me. Went down to basement and hauled up old magic chest from childhood. Faded marker in my old handwriting on lid of chest: PRIVATE STAY AWAY JANET!!! Many fights with Janet, accused her of spying many times, usually furious with her. Still, loved her a lot. Great sister in most ways. Discovered later that she was imaginary. Tough time for me, for parents too. Me: You don't even care that Janet's dead. Them: But Janet's not dead. There is no Janet. Me: Because you murdered her.

Sifted through contents of chest. Decks of cards, handkerchiefs, Cape of Invisibility. Old drawings for tricks I couldn't remember. Nonworking version of Marvelous Orange Tree, which Janet called Non-Marvelous Orange Tree.

What is it that makes us smile, seeing things from childhood? And then feel kind of sad, even before smile is gone. Kind of like, this is who you were, remember? But not anymore. Not anymore.

Poured margarita, poured Bo dogarita. Not really special drink for Bo, just plain water. Sat outside and began reading *Learn French in a Day!* Practiced on Bo, who I called Pierre. Kept phone nearby, just in case.

Was in the middle of telling Pierre an important fact about Marie's hair when phone rang. Answered and said, Philip!

I know it's been awhile since I've called, he said.

I told him I knew he was busy. Told him I felt like we'd been "corresponding" through voice-mail messages, which are like today's version of old-fashioned letters, honest and reflective. Or like letters written to person who can't respond, trapped in rubble maybe, but can still read and appreciate letters. You wonder: Why can't mail delivery person save this person from rubble while delivering reflective old-fashioned letters? But no, can't. Can only keep delivering letters.

That's great, he said. So listen, I wouldn't even bring this up if it weren't an emergency. I feel bad asking at all, considering, you know. But Kady? She's in a bad spot right now, Dad.

Okay, I said. Sure, son. Tell me what's going on.

He said she's been taking a lot of heat from other kids at school due to wooden arm. Is called Peg, and classmates have spread rumor she is descended from pirates and probably has syphilis. Other prosthetic kids at school have titanium arms and robotic arms wired directly to central nervous system.

I said I didn't realize there were so many kids with prosthetic arms in preschool.

She's sunk into a terrible depression, he said. Is developing stump infection due to low-quality wood in prosthetic. Really needs a new arm but they can't afford one, insurance won't cover. Considered cosmetic!

That's horrible, I said.

She's seeing a therapist, he said. To cope with dark thoughts. Do you want her to have dark thoughts?

No, I said. Of course not!

He said the therapist sessions weren't covered either, but he was paying out of pocket. What else could he do, he said, except give her what she needed?

I tried to focus. Wished I hadn't had margarita. Seemed like perfect time to be clear-headed. Instead, still thinking about mail delivery person, refusing to save Philip from rubble.

He said, I've never begged before. Do I really need to beg? Is that what you want? Because if that's what I need to do, then okay. Okay, Dad. I love my daughter and I'm begging. Are you happy?

I asked how much.

The titanium arm or the good one, the one that's wired to the central nervous system?

I swallowed and said, Well tell me about both of them.

He told me.

Started sweating. Philip, I said. I'm sorry.

Forget it. Listen, I've got to go. Kady's screaming.

Maybe your mom, I said, but didn't get any farther than that. His *mom*, he said, had already gone above and beyond for him and for his family. Had raised Margot and him after the divorce, bailed him out of jail during that period when he was stealing things, later paid his way through rehab. He wouldn't dream of asking her for more help. Was only asking me because he thought maybe I would want to do this. If not for him, then for Kady. Wasn't Kady an innocent? Maybe he'd fucked everything up and disappointed me, he said. But what had Kady ever done to anyone? Why did she deserve to suffer and die? Just because he was a screwup and couldn't afford to give her the care that she needed?

Sun was going down, and someone set off fireworks. Bo grabbed lounge pad in teeth, started eating. I yelled at him to stop.

Who's Pierre? Philip asked. Suspicious.

I explained that Pierre was Bo, Bo was Pierre.

He said, I don't know why I even asked. Then hung up.

Went inside and sat down at computer. Checked 401k, somewhat depressing. Should have saved more, should have started saving before fortieth birthday. Could maybe pay for one-fourth of arm, after withdrawal penalty. What is one-fourth of arm? Just shoulder, probably, plus partial bicep. Imagined Kady staring down at robotic shoulder connected to rotting wooden arm, then reaching sadly for razor blade. Awful. Logged in to banking site. Filled out quick-loan application, provided home equity details and social security number and projected lifetime earning potential. Hit submit. We'll have an answer for you in moments! Cartoon millionaire holding bag marked with dollar sign, tap-dancing on-screen.

More fireworks. Dog moaned and looked for place to throw up.

Tapped fingers on desk, watching cartoon millionaire. Cartoon millionaire stopped dancing, got in limousine and drove away, disappeared in puff of smoke. Replaced with single word, giant black letters

Fierce Pretty Things

on white screen. NO. Then letters sprouted little feet, followed million-aire offscreen, dancing.

Called Philip back, no answer. Called Margot. When I couldn't reach her, went to her blog. Read message that she was offline to celebrate life of her beloved father, Brian David Winston. Clicked on Contact Me! page and left her a note. It's me, it's Mike, it's Uncle Mike. Call if you can. If you want to!

Cleaned up Bo's mess. Kept remembering day I explained bankruptcy situation to kids. Gwen: Kids, Gelato Man has something to tell you. Philip, in middle school, looking at me as I talked about need to tighten our belts, lead simple unfettered lives, et cetera. Demanding to know how I'd let this happen, why I couldn't have done more, why I couldn't have worked harder. I said sometimes you just make mistakes, that's all, no matter how hard you try, and he yelled then what's the fucking point of trying. What's the fucking point of anything? Then ran off, tried to lock himself in bedroom. Except lock never worked, so had to push heavy dresser across doorway to keep us out, which took some time. Another source of fury for Philip. Waited politely outside bedroom while he moved dresser, then tried to explain. I wish you were dead, Philip said. Out of breath from moving dresser, half sobbing. I said, You don't really wish that, and I forgive you. And he said, Oh, Dad, but I do.

* * *

Sat on front porch that night with Marvelous Orange Tree. Found in old magic book as a kid, tried to recreate. Idea is to make beautiful woman's handkerchief vanish, then reappear inside magically blooming orange tree, suspended by butterfly wings. Jaw-dropping spectacle, leaves audience in tears. Audience thinks, *Thank you, magician, for this gift.* Except it never worked. Could never get gears working right, made horrible sound completely different from sound real orange tree makes. Embarrassed, told Janet sound was butterflies caught in gears, screaming. Janet burst into tears, wouldn't speak to me for weeks.

Could sell magic chest, maybe. For how much? Not enough, not with broken Marvelous Orange Tree that sounded like screaming butterflies.

Maybe go on tour, perform at local events. Mike the Magnificent Returns! Assume four shows a weekend. Not reasonable, considering lack of experience, but assume anyway. Fifty dollars a show. Or a hundred? Say fifty. Two hundred a week, fifty weeks a year, that's ten thousand. Five more years to raise money for new arm wired directly to Kady's central nervous system. Imagined calling Philip, telling him plan. Thanks, Dad! Only five more years of stump infections and dark thoughts for Kady.

Went inside and put Orange Tree back in chest. Found small square envelope taped to underside of lid. Inside was a faded sheet of construction paper, folded in quarters. A crayon drawing. Our family as giant sunflowers, standing in front of house. Margot dancing, Philip flexing stick sunflower muscles. Me with big goofy smile, weird teeth. Gwen as nearby rain cloud. ("Just kidding!" underneath cloud, in Margot's handwriting.) Signed at the bottom by both of them.

Looked at envelope again. Something written there in pencil, the letters faded, almost gone.

FOR WHEN YOU NEED IT.

* * *

Dreamed that night of the train station. Both kids were with me. Stay close, I said. Felt sudden, horrible sense of dread. Knew what was coming. Heart pounding. Overcome by profound sense of tragic inevitability, but couldn't stop moving.

Rounded the corner and he was there. Like in real life, holding a gun. Only in dream it wasn't a gun, just gooseneck gourd. But in dream world, such gourds incredibly deadly. Just do as I say and nobody gets hurt. Brandishing gourd in menacing way.

The world slowed down, became almost still. A weird and beautiful sunset on the horizon. Margot looked up at me. Philip too. Clutching model airplane. So beautiful, both of them. So sweet and undamaged. Just waiting for me, trusting. Was overwhelmed by love for them, from them. Felt powerful and certain of everything, of what to do. Maybe for first time. Knocked mugger to the sidewalk and began beating him. Like wild person, like animal protecting its young. Heart pounding as mugger's face turned to mush underneath me. So much blood. Pushed thumbs into mugger's eye sockets and felt adrenaline-fueled joy. Lifted mugger's head and bashed it into pavement, again and again. At last Philip knelt down next to me and held out a book of matches. Margot, pouring the gasoline.

Didn't remember dream right away when I woke up. But felt calm, happy. Certain. Went to the kitchen and searched through recycling bin until I found letter from Retirement Recruiters.

* * *

Recruiter was friendly and professional, named Ellis. Younger than me, but very accomplished, wall covered in diplomas.

He explained everything. Very patient. Living to a hundred or a hundred and fifty is great, he said, sure, if you have the money. Otherwise not so great. Otherwise, maybe long life really just sad, costly decline. Still get diseases, still spend time in hospital, losing faculties, not working. Who pays for care? Who pays for miracle cures? Children and grandchildren pay, society pays. Pretty soon world is full of unproductive old people supported by children and grandchildren. And by taxes on the rich, who make everything possible. What kind of world is that for old rich person who just wants to enjoy long life earned through simple hard work? What kind of world is that for children and grandchildren, who only want same chance at long, happy life?

Handed me brochure. *Take One for the Team.* Get out of the game early, he said, and everybody wins. Of course your beneficiaries will receive maximum payout due to your young age, magnitude of your sacrifice, et cetera. But that wasn't most important thing. Most important thing, he said, was my commitment to children, grandchildren, et cetera, giving them chance at something better. He showed me photographs of crowds in front of Grand Wall of Heroes in Times Square, names carved in diamond in granite wall, designed to catch final rays of sunset and blaze like stars for all eternity.

Our local version maybe not as elaborate, he said, maybe name would only flash on simple digital screen below time and temperature, every few months. But is that what motivates heroes? Real heroes not concerned with name blazing like star for all eternity on Grand Wall of Heroes, he said. Important thing is that I'd be beloved. Or not important thing, exactly, but a nice thing, sure, important thing being my commitment to children, grandchildren, humanity, et cetera. Still, nice to be beloved. The end's going to come sooner or later. When bell finally tolls, how many can truly say they were beloved?

I stared down at the contract. Thought about little sunflower family. Just wanted to do the right thing for once.

Okay, I said.

After signing, I asked how long.

A whole week, Ellis said. Enjoy it! Set your affairs in order, of course. But have fun. Gather ye rosebuds. Spend your money, take a trip, get laid! You've earned it!

And in a week, I said, I come back here and die?

Painlessly, he said, and with a heart at peace! What more could you want? What more could anyone want?

I agreed. Could never want any more than that.

* * *

Found Kozma on front porch when I got home, sitting with Bo.

He was in my backyard, Kozma said. I think he ate an inflatable raft?

I said I was sorry and thanked him, and let Bo back inside. Kozma walked in behind us and said milk would be really good, and I agreed that it would be. Then understood what he meant, and walked to the kitchen to get milk while he wandered around the house.

Brought two glasses of milk to the living room. Kozma was sitting on the floor with Bo, looking at magic chest. Eyes wide.

It's like from olden times, he said.

You can open it, I said. It's mostly junk.

He looked at the writing on the lid, STAY AWAY, et cetera. He asked, Who's Janet?

I explained.

Always spying on you, he said. I get it.

He opened the chest and pulled out Marvelous Orange Tree. I told him how it was supposed to work, re: handkerchief, butterflies,

Fierce Pretty Things

everyone's jaw dropping to the floor. He found the hidden crank and turned it, and we both cringed.

Still, he said. It could work, right?

I said I always thought so.

He pulled out other things, asked questions. I showed him Cups and Balls, vanishing coin, a few card tricks. How to palm. Easy stuff, far as I ever got. He picked up the Cape of Invisibility and blinked at me. From when I first started learning, I said, before I knew how anything worked. Said I thought maybe a thing could just have magic in it, with no tricks. He tied the cape around his neck and I gasped, demanded that Bo tell me this instant what he'd done with Kozma. Bo wagged his tail while Kozma laughed.

What's this, he said. Pulled out a poster that had been rolled up and tied with a ribbon. He unrolled it and spread it across the floor. Looked like an old treasure map, taped together in a hundred places.

You drew this? he asked, and I nodded. A skiff, he said. And you got everything labeled.

I looked down, remembered. Rub rails, tackle locker, flag holder for Jolly Roger, et cetera. *The Grand Adventure* written across the transom in three-dimensional letters, words curving up and down like ocean waves.

Kozma whispered the boat's name. Did you ever build it? he asked.

I said I brought the drawing to my dad so we could build it together. Had seen photograph of him and Pop-Pop in similar boat from back when he was a boy. My dad stared at the drawing for a long time. Then said, You want to know what a grand adventure is? It's when you go to work at the cannery when you're fifteen and then spend the next fifty years in the same place, coming home every night smelling like fish guts with your palms cut to pieces from the cannery knives. Cut yourself so many times that the nerves are dead and you can't hold a cup of coffee without dropping it. You grow old. You think at least you'll get to retire and spend golden years alongside loving companion. Retirement comes, you go out to mall with Grandmom to celebrate, except Grandmom has heart attack while eating bowl of macaroni salad. You grab defibrillator from wall and run back to save her, only can't hold defibrillator due to nerve damage in hands. Defibrillator drops stupidly to floor and she dies, face covered in macaroni. That's the grand adventure of life! Then he tore up the drawing.

Okay, Kozma said. Well that's a horrible story.

I said he was just trying to teach me.

Kozma said, Well he didn't have to say it like that. Nobody has to talk to his boy like that.

I felt tired. Told Kozma I needed to lay down for a bit. He said goodbye to Bo and walked to the door, then realized he was still wearing Cape of Invisibility and started taking it off.

Keep it, I said.

He nodded and said thanks. Started to leave, then said, Maybe he was just having a bad day when he told you that. Maybe he didn't mean it, and later on he regretted saying that to you.

I told him to be careful going home. Reminded him cars couldn't see him due to Cape of Invisibility, and he smiled.

Sat alone for the rest of day, thinking.

Finally called kids. Margot touched by news, said I was always favorite uncle. Admitted she secretly imagined sometimes that she was my daughter, wondered what that would have been like. Maybe terrible, she said. Maybe better to only be a fantasy, to be able to say goodbye and feel this love for me as beloved uncle.

Philip confused, then disbelieving. Then overcome with emotion as he realized Kady would soon have arm wired directly to nervous system. Became friendlier, chatty. Told funny, heartwarming stories about Kady. Even asked about job at recycling plant, and about Bo.

We should get together, he said. For dinner.

I said I'd love that, but I knew he was busy.

He said that was nonsense. Pointed out that we lived five miles from each other. He said since my last day was Saturday, maybe we could have dinner on Friday at a nice restaurant in the city? I said that would be great, son.

Tried to lie down for a nap but the phone kept ringing. From cousins, neighbors, old friends. Just calling to thank me for my service. Such kindness from them, from all of them.

Fierce Pretty Things

It was dark when the last call ended. Sat with Bo on the couch, staring at magic chest. Thought about what recruiter had said: set your affairs in order. Had an idea.

Walked with Bo to the Judge's house. Kozma answered the door in his pajamas, still wearing cape.

I said I brought you something, if you want it. Showed him what I'd brought: magic chest, strapped to Philip's old Radio Flyer wagon.

He backed up a step. Why? he said.

Judge appeared in the doorway and put his hand on Kozma's shoulder. Tall, silver hair. Carved face, full of muscles. More muscles in face than I had in entire body. Introduced myself and tried to explain reason for appearance, but Judge stopped me and thrust giant granite hand toward me. An absolute honor to meet you, he said. Shook my hand and repeated: an absolute honor, sir!

Well, I said, looking down at his boy. Kozma confused, but happy. I said, I brought this for your boy. Just some old stuff I thought he might like.

Ah, said the Judge. Putting away childish things?

I said I guessed so. Kozma still beaming, eyes going back and forth. I said I had to get going, shook hands again with Judge. Waved at Kozma as I left.

Went home, feeling good. Spent next two hours in basement, throwing things away. Found some old toys from when kids were very young, set aside in box for Kady. Made list of things to give to charity, small list due to not having many things worth giving to charity. Finally turned off basement light, went upstairs to bed. Picked up *Great Gatsby*. Had been reading for months. Had always been slow reader, which now seemed unfortunate. Still, liked book. Hoping things worked out for Gatsby, Daisy.

Woke up before the dawn, earliest I'd been awake in years. Got dressed and walked outside with Bo as the sky changed color. Sat in field at Civil War park and watched the sun come up over the trees. Dawn wind rustled the leaves, washing over me and Bo. Cried a little. Just tired, probably. Just a little tired.

Spent much of day clearing out house and taking breaks to read *Gatsby*. Took Bo out after dinner and saw Kozma in field at Civil War park again. Not flying kite this time, just sitting in grass, wearing Cape of Invisibility. I waved until he saw me but he stormed off into the trees. Later, found a note under the front door.

My dad told me what you did. I think I hate you right now but I'm not sure because I'm pretty bad upset. But maybe I hate you. K.

* * *

On Monday I showed up early at work.

Why are you here? Toby asked.

I said I couldn't sleep.

No, he said. Why are you here at all? You ought to be celebrating! He shook his head. If I were you I'd never stop drinking and getting blowjobs and screaming. And maybe doing cocaine. I'd be doing all those things twenty-four hours a day until they shot me full of dope and I was dead.

I said I didn't think anyone really wanted to give someone a blowjob when he's screaming and doing cocaine, and Toby said he knew someone who did. I said thanks but I just wanted to go to work. He shrugged and said, Okay, weirdo!

Spent rest of day writing copy for company website and blog. Exciting time due to recent acquisition of new twin screw extruder, although excitement offset by last month's explosion. Tough job, balancing excitement versus overwhelming grief. Handed first draft to Mitch, senior web copywriter.

Whatever, Mitch said. Threw story in garbage. I hear you're going to die, he said.

We're all going to die, I said.

Whatever. Hope there's a good reason.

I told him about Kady's wooden arm, et cetera.

A suicidal four-year-old with a wooden arm, he said. That's great. What's the real reason?

I said I needed to get back to work.

Fierce Pretty Things

Later, saw Meg in break room. She walked toward me and I assumed she didn't see me as usual, so I jumped out of the way, crashed into vending machine.

She said, I know you hate me, but you don't have to jump like that. My cloudy eye isn't going to eat you. I heard what you're doing, and I just wanted to say that I'm sorry I horrified you so much with my cloudy eye.

I rubbed my shoulder and tried to say that was all wrong, that I loved her cloudy eye. But she shook her head before I could finish and said there was no point denying it. Said she could tell by the weird thing I did with my mouth whenever I looked her in the cloudy eye. I said that was just the way I smiled and I showed her, and she said, Oh, Jesus, well that explains it.

Well, I said.

We both looked down at our feet.

Maybe in the next life, ha ha, I said.

She said, That's just really sad. Why would you make a joke like that?

I said I was just uncomfortable because I didn't know what to say.

So that's okay, she said. You don't have to know. You can just not say anything sometimes.

I blinked, said nothing.

Well okay, she said. Goodbye, I guess.

* * *

Tried to enjoy my last week on earth. But worried about Kozma. Worried he was angry with me, thought less of me for decision.

Woke up before dawn each morning. Not sleeping anyway. Went out with Bo each day to sit in the field and watch sunrise. Then, when sunrise was over, felt moment of great peace. Followed by moment of paralyzing terror. Tried to focus on first thing.

Read *Gatsby* in the evenings. Felt love for all of them, even Daisy, who was crazy. Why cry about shirts? But made sense, too, didn't it? Had to admit pile of beautiful shirts on bed was maybe saddest thing in the world. Such fragile people. A little worried wasn't going to finish the book but didn't want to read any faster. Maybe didn't totally want to get to the end either.

Took Bo out for walks in the evening and kept eye out for Kozma. No sign of him, but on Wednesday I noticed flyers pinned up around the neighborhood. Stopped and read one.

EXPERIENCE TERROR AND DELIGHT
WITH KOZMA THE MAGNIFICENT!
SAT 10 A.M., FREE OF CHARGE
3902 LIBERTY COURT
(BACKYARD SHED, KNOCK TWICE)

Someone had written FUCKFACE! in marker through the middle of the flyer, so I pulled it down. Folded it and put it in my pocket, took Bo home.

Stopped at bank after work on Thursday and withdrew cash. Bank teller recognized me and smiled. Going out with a bang? she said. I smiled back. At home, found a bag and stuffed most of cash inside. Not a fortune, but it was something. Walked down path that led beneath the bridge. Bridge Guy was huddled up in sleeping bag, and I didn't want to wake him. Left bag on the ground along with note: *Thank you for your service.*

On Friday I called Philip to make sure we were still meeting for dinner. He didn't answer, but I went to the restaurant anyway. Waited for an hour. Ordered a drink, first drink all week. Called him again, still no answer. Had another drink, then left.

House was dark when I got home. Thought I'd left the light on for Bo. Unlocked the door and stepped inside and the whole place came to life. Live music playing, confetti everywhere. Filled with people, smiling faces everywhere, everyone stepping forward to shake my hand. Everyone laughing, pouring champagne. Giant blown-up photograph of me on easel in living room, surrounded by flowers.

Margot kissed me, and I put my head down. Shaken.

Sorry I missed dinner, Philip said.

Asked if Kady was here and he said, Sorry, she had a thing tonight, but she really wanted to come. But she says you're the greatest!

I hugged him tight.

Party was wonderful, dreamlike. Toby and Meg showed up from work, and the Stintons and the Quincys were both there. Lots of singing, children running from room to room. Didn't know who they were, but nice to see anyway. Toby played "For He's a Jolly Good Fellow" on harmonica while the whole room sang along. Everyone so kind and grateful. Thank you, they said, over and over. Thank you, Mike.

When the party ended, sat in backyard with Margot and Philip. World glowed under a full moon. We talked in low voices about their childhood, about things they remembered. About little things that didn't mean anything. I told them about reading *Gatsby*, and Margot asked what I thought so far, and I said I liked it very much. She said me too, and then she stared at the ground and was quiet for a long time.

Dreamed that night about my dad and *The Grand Adventure*. Hands shaking as I showed him the drawing. Knew it was good but wanted him to love it. Wanted it to fill him with wonder, I guess, like in an after-school television special. Could almost hear soaring after-school-special piano music playing, in dream. Then he took drawing in his hands and tore it to pieces and stomped off to his bedroom.

I picked up the pieces and went down the hall. Not a kid anymore in the dream. Just me, just tired middle-aged man. Pushed the door open and found him sitting on edge of bed with his face in his hands. I wanted to say something to him then, maybe put arm around him. But I didn't. Pulled the door shut and let him be.

* * *

I woke up groggy, staring into Bo's face, Bo hopping from leg to leg, impatient. Checked the clock and said, Shit. Missed the sunrise.

Later, outside with Bo, stepped on another of Kozma's flyers. Checked watch and said shit again, then raced over to the Judge's house.

Went around back and didn't see anyone, so walked over to big shed in the back. Looked at watch—10:10. I knocked twice.

Kozma answered. Wearing black pajamas, black T-shirt, and Cape of Invisibility.

He looked up at me. Nobody came, he said.

We came, I said. Bo and me.

Kozma said, Well you might as well come in. He'd set up a small wooden platform in front of an old sofa. I sat down with Bo. He flipped off the lights and stepped onto platform, shone flashlight up at his face. Gave little introduction about all this being illusion, about how we should suppress natural instinctive terror we in the audience may feel, et cetera.

Started with Four Burglars. Nice little story from Kozma, said jacks only became burglars due to grievous oppression. Terrible commotion after king's men alerted, jacks had to escape to castle roof for helicopter escape. At the end he turned over first three cards to reveal burglars. Last card was eight of hearts instead of jack of spades. Felt heart sink for him because he'd practiced so much. But Kozma shrugged and said maybe fourth burglar fell in love with two of clubs and decided to stick around.

After that he did variations of Miser's Dream and Gypsy Thread and French Drop and a few more card tricks. Asked for volunteer each time, pretended to pick me out of crowd. You, sir, with the dog. Told crazy story during each trick, always with odd, sweet twist. So Miser also lonely werewolf saving up money to buy shoes for son's wedding, kept destroying shoes each full moon due to werewolf transformation. And Gypsy long-lost daughter of King of Hearts, who had just been robbed by Four Burglars. Et cetera. Everything linked together in funny, sad way.

At the end he brought out the Orange Tree.

I held my breath, and Kozma smiled. I didn't figure it out, he said. But for a second you believed I did, right?

Laughed and said he was already a better magician than I ever was.

I'll get better, he said. Next time. Then he looked away and started cleaning up his little stage. I asked him if he'd take Bo for me. He stopped and stared at me, thinking. Then said, You can't leave until you find a home for him, right?

I said that was true, and he said, Then no.

Okay, I said. I understand. Well I should go, son.

Don't know why I called him that. Walked to the door of the shed and Bo trotted after me, but Kozma stopped us.

Okay, he said. I'll watch after him. Somebody's got to, right?

I said that was true.

Just go, he said. Don't say goodbye or else I'll change my mind.

I left. When I got home, reached into pocket for keys. Found jack of clubs, with two words written across the top.

BYE MIKE.

*　*　*

Spent last few hours thinking, reading. Realized at five o'clock I didn't have time to finish *Gatsby* so called Margot to ask how it ended but she didn't answer. Then called Philip. He answered but said he was running out, asked if it was important. I said no, not really. I said to tell Kady goodbye for me, and he said he'd already done that.

Finally went to get dressed. Wasn't totally sure what was appropriate but didn't want to look like slob. Settled on khakis, clean shirt, navy blazer from college. Examined self in mirror. Looked like I was going to dinner on cruise ship.

Drove very slowly. Each mile slower than the last.

Thinking about Philip. Hated weakness so much. Hated to be poor, to have nothing, to be nothing. Never understood how much he hated it. Should have done more somehow. Thought there had to be something more I could give, more than this. Philip just fucked up kid, now fucked up adult. Margot too. My fault. Made too many mistakes. Didn't realize I only got one chance to be a good dad. No one tells you: only one chance. Too late now maybe. But why? Why would it ever be too late to be good? To fix things?

Cars piling up behind me, honking.

I pulled over to shoulder.

More honking, screaming.

Called recruiter's office.

The man of the hour! he said.

Hypothetically, I said, what happens if I don't show up?

He set the phone down for a few seconds. Heard him talking to someone else in the office. Then: I don't think I heard you, Mike. The connection? Is kind of bad?

I'm not doing it, I said.

He said that he had to advise me against that course of action. Reminded me that once six o'clock rolled around, I would technically be dead. He said, Do you really want to be a Runner? Put your family through that? They won't see a dime of the bounty when you're hunted down.

I said there has to be some other way.

You signed a contract, he said. He put the phone aside again, said something else I couldn't hear. Then: Look, let's go over the options in person. How about you swing by?

I said I thought there weren't any options.

Ha ha, he said. Where are you exactly?

I hung up. Called Philip back, tried to explain. You've got to be kidding, he said, right? Have you forgotten Kady? Just last night, for the love of God, Dad, the stump infection—

I said I knew Kady wasn't real. He'd made her up the same way I'd made Janet up. I told him I wasn't mad. Just tell me, I said. Tell me what's going on. We can figure it out. Trust me, son.

Well, he said. Jesus, wow, Dad. Of course, that's the answer, not sure why I didn't see that before. I'm sure I can work things out with my business acquaintances now that I know I can trust you! Not sure why I didn't realize that before, instead of wasting my time hating your guts and waiting for you to die.

Philip, I said, there's a way out. I can help you. That's what fathers do. He made a sound that was like a snort, except also terrible and sad. Then hung up on me.

Pulled car into Lucky's and went inside. Shaken by conversation with Philip, just needed to sit and figure things out. Checked wallet and realized money was gone, but bartender smiled and said no charge for me. A true honor to meet me, he said.

I groaned.

The TV flashed with a news update. My face, alongside graphic showing stick figure running from giant fist holding scales of justice. Scales of justice filled with crying stick children. Newsperson explained bounty rules, full payout to whoever took me down, et cetera. Good luck, he said, and Godspeed.

Bartender reached slowly under bar, and I fled.

Took some time to get back to my neighborhood. People out in the streets with guns, knives, torches. Not sure why torches. But had to stay in shadows, follow back roads. Finally came to my street. Growing dark, melancholy skies. Maybe just imagination. Or maybe skies always looked that way, not sure.

Saw house and stopped. Shadows moving on the front porch. Stinton, maybe, and Quincy. Metal flashed in the lamplight.

Moved off sidewalk and crouched beside bushes. Someone tapped me on the shoulder. I turned and waited for head to explode.

Come with me, Kozma said.

*   *   *

Spent evening in Kozma's shed.

He told me his plan. I'd have to lay low for a while, he said. In the evenings we'd practice our act, coming up with new tricks and working on our patter. We'd have to come up with a good name, too, something to inspire wonder and dread. During the day, he said, he'd help me build the ship.

What ship, I said.

He pointed. My taped sketch for *The Grand Adventure* was hanging on the back wall, next to a US map. He said we'd head south once we reached the Mississippi. Perform our act in small villages, build up a name for ourselves. Become legendary figures of danger and mystery. The locals would take blood oaths to protect us.

I stared at the drawing and map for some time. Finally said, Then we'd better practice an awful lot, I guess.

Kozma beamed.

We stayed up late. Talked about our upcoming adventures, which always ended with a daring escape through sewer tunnels, secret catacombs, et cetera. Discussed how to include Bo in our act, and what colors we'd paint the ship. Finally Kozma yawned, and I said he ought to get to bed.

He nodded and looked toward the door. Well, he said, it's nice to think about, isn't it?

It is, I said. Don't think even he really believed it was something we would do, but still. The thought of it. Setting out like that. As if everything was new again.

Tomorrow we'll come up with a good name, he said. Standing by the door now, hesitating.

Don't worry, I said. Go to sleep.

Almost hugged him then, but didn't. Not my place.

Night, he said.

* * *

Didn't sleep. Rain started around midnight, pounding against shed roof. Now and then heard helicopters passing overhead.

Stared up at shed roof and thought about what would happen. Someone would find me soon. Gun me down in shed, probably splatter blood all over magic chest and sketch of *The Grand Adventure*. Maybe splatter brains too. Kozma would run out, find me dead, brains splattered, et cetera. Would have horrible picture of my brains on shed floor stuck in his mind forever, and feel like he hadn't done enough. Would spend rest of days thinking life was tragic and filled with unexpected horror.

Had to leave.

Stood up as the shed door opened and the Judge walked in. Dripping wet, holding a rifle. He stared at me, at everything in the shed. Like he'd never walked in here before. Finally brought his eyes back to me, leveled rifle at my chest.

His hands shook. Never saw anyone look so old.

I dropped down to my knees and closed my eyes.

Get up, he said. Get up! He stepped out of the way and jerked the rifle at the open doorway. His face twisted. Run, he roared.

I ran out into the rain, into the empty street. Helicopter passed by again, shining spotlight down. I headed down beneath the bridge.

Bridge Guy was still wrapped in his blanket, but his body was half in the rain, not moving. Walked closer and asked if he was okay. He wasn't. Obviously dead. Not Bridge Guy anymore, just rotting meat lying in the rain. Shouldn't have given him money. Probably bought heroin, overdosed, crawled back down here to die. Gwen always said not to give money to homeless for exactly that reason. Smart Gwen, terrible Gwen.

Backed away and stumbled over something. The bag I left, still filled with money. Felt relieved because hadn't contributed to Bridge Guy's heroin overdose. He just died, that's all. Just died all alone under bridge, despite bag of money a few feet away.

Found dry spot far away from corpse and curled up into ball, listened to helicopter as it passed back and forth. Last thing I saw before falling asleep was bridge graffiti, lit by helicopter spotlight.

I WAS HERE, it said.

*   *   *

When I woke up the rain was gone. Flies buzzed around Bridge Guy. I called 911 and said I wanted to report the death of a homeless man under the bridge, and the operator said why. I hung up.

It was still early. I climbed up the path and walked through the streets. Quiet, everyone home for the holiday. Walked past the Judge's house, Stinton's place. My own house was already boarded up.

Came to the Civil War park. Sun was still rising through the eastern trees. Thought about the Judge, letting me go. For his boy, who made no sense to him. And still he let me go. I called Philip. Told him where I was, and then said goodbye. Threw the phone into the trees. Then went out into the field and knelt down in the dawn shadows. Felt at peace. Just glad I was here. Glad I'd ever been here.

Somewhere a car door slammed. I rose up straight.

The ground next to me came to life. Kozma sprang up. Holding his cape wide, laughing. It works! he shrieked. I'm invisible! We're invisible! And he leaned down to envelop me. Kozma the Magnificent.

There just wasn't any time.

First bullet struck me in the back. Heard the second blast as Kozma fell into my arms, but didn't feel anything. Rolled onto the ground with Kozma and tried to cover him. Felt something pop in back of head. Couldn't see anything from right eye, but left eye pretty good. Left eye good enough to see Kozma wasn't doing great. Face pale, already in shock. Listened for his breathing but hard to hear anything. Hard to think clearly. So much blood on both of us.

Oh Jesus, someone behind me said.

Turned and looked with good left eye. Didn't need to say anything. He already knew. Poor Philip.

Son, I said. Give me the gun.

He didn't move. Breathing hard. Staring at Kozma, at me. So lost.

Now! I yelled, and finally he handed me the gun. Now run, I said. Please, Philip, run.

And he ran.

Looked down at Kozma. All the color leaving his face, but he was still awake. Confused. Scared. A helicopter passed overhead and sirens sounded.

He cried and asked for his dad. Just like any little boy, just wanted his dad. Just wanted to be safe, that's all. I brushed his hair back and told him he was good. I said his dad was coming soon. Helicopter passed by again. Heard voices yelling but couldn't see anything anymore. Felt the sun burst over the trees and held Kozma's hand. With the other hand I raised the gun high. Told Kozma again that his dad was coming. Someone charged toward us through the trees. I hoped it was him. Hoped that just this once I got it right, and it was him.

8

Xiomara

Friday afternoon, 3:15 p.m. Traffic hums merrily along as the week-end approaches. Songbirds overhead are in full voice. Far beyond the suburban streets, high in the hills, the earth is abloom with color. The world's every breeze carries upon it the scent and the promise of summer, et cetera, et cetera.

And yet. Does the universe not teeter on the very brink of destruction?

Yes. Yes, it does teeter, on that exact brink.

Charlie pauses with one foot in the air. Poised in mid-footfall above the narrow curb, he wonders if just maybe the universe, in fact, *totters* on the brink, et cetera. The whole teeters versus totters question. A classic question, sure, a question for the ages: *but*. Come on, man.

This is no time to get distracted. Not with so much on the line vis-à-vis the universe, imminent destruction of. Charlie's admittedly wide feet are almost as wide as the curb, and it's critical that he not brush even the edge of his shoe against that neighboring sidewalk there. That's how big this is. How big? Try eschatologically big. Try end-of-times big. That's all we're talking about here. Despite the traffic, songbirds, world being abloom with color, et cetera. Despite the rest of the world being oblivious to the tightrope walk—no, the *death waltz*, if by death you mean the heat-death of the universe—that Charlie is walking, or rather waltzing, here.

His phone buzzes, and then. Oops. He whips his head around to make sure the destruction of the universe has gone unwitnessed by his eighth-grade classmates. Checks his message.

Working late again, sorry!

He taps back, *De nada, milady*. Which always makes Xiomara smile. Ah, *mijo*, she says. Such a Casanova! You talk to all the girls like that? To which Charlie is like, ha ha, yes? The last time he talked to a girl other than Xiomara was last November. The girl in question being Trish Mackey, fabled Trish Mackey of the azure eyes that have tormented Charlie's dreams since kindergarten, who one day in November dropped her notebook in the hallway on the way (*en route*) to Social Studies. At which point Charlie, seized by an instinct so powerful, no, so primordial that questioning it would have been *anathema* (yes!), grabbed the notebook from the floor and took off after her at full speed, which for Charlie wasn't exceptionally fast, no, but still left him out of breath by the time he reached her, sweating, let's just say, profusely, stomach lurching just a bit more than one would consider the normal amount of lurching. And then, head bowed just so as he presented the notebook, a knight laying the Grail before the queen, eyes on Trish Mackey's pretty gold-painted toenails showing through her designer flip-flops, on which Charlie was trying with all of his thirteen-year-old might to neither sweat nor vomit, he proclaimed: *Your scroll, milady.*

A great story right up until that exact point. And then, not so much. Then: screaming, running, a certain not insignificant amount of shame.

Buzz. *Beso grande. Late bus? Or maybe ride w/SteveO?* And then some kind of crazy-eye emoji thing, what Xiomara calls her trademark.

He taps, *No problema. Hugs.* Best to keep old Steve-O out of this. Xiomara's been telling him to invite the legendary Steve-O to dinner for the last three months, which means that Steve-O's days might, sadly, be numbered. Certain difficult decisions have to be made. Possibly Steve-O's heading to China as part of a foreign-exchange program, or he's suffering from memory loss after that spectacular fall from the water tower. Foreshadowed, of course, by comments Charlie has lately made over Sunday Sundaes with Xiomara: Yeah, old Steve-O can't stop talking about China! Everything's Tiananmen Square and the Falun Gong with this guy! Also: Steve-O's been acting kind of weird, said some crazy things to me in homeroom. Maybe that fall last week affected him more than he's let on, ha ha. But a sad ha ha. A tragicomic ha ha. Followed by a day or two of Charlie moping around, distracted by the tiff with old Steve-O, with whom he'd become pretty damn close. Such bad luck with friends, *chiquito*—Xiomara shaking her head—and after that thing with Big John's family going into the Witness Protection Program last year.

Buzz. *Will bring chicken tacos. L8r pooh bear.* Crazy-eye thing.

Pooh Bear—her name for him. Maybe not the absolute most flattering nickname. Maybe a nickname that caused him a few problems after he left his phone in Algebra class and Alan Mears found it. For a few days he was called Pooh Bear by everyone, including Trish Mackey, which would've been bad enough. Ah, but then. Then Alan's friend Miggs suggested a better name: Shit Bear. Which caught on so, so quickly.

Xiomara doesn't know this. She calls him Pooh Bear, she says, because he never gets angry or upset. Because he's always sweet, always smiling, always gentle. Oh, if she only knew. For example: Just this morning, after Charlie finished reading aloud his poem, "When to the Silence (I Summon Thy Joyful Roar)," Alan called out *Shit bear shit bear shit-shit-shit.* Which was stupid and not even in iambic pentameter, and what did it even mean? But everyone laughed and even the teacher smiled, and for an instant Charlie was filled with the most bilious (yes!) hatred, and a desire for biblical-level vengeance. For an instant he wanted Alan Mears to, like, explode. Or no, not explode. Maybe just have a stroke. And be disabled and not be able to walk or speak! Yes! And to drool everywhere, so that everyone in class pointed and said nasty things like *Drooly Drooly Alan Mears!* Also nastier things, too, probably. But then Charlie pictured Alan's half-paralyzed face, drool running down onto his wheelchair, kids laughing, Alan staring at the floor in shame. Alan's mother wiping his face for him, feeding him, changing his diaper because he's just constantly pooping for some reason, and bathing him like a toddler. And crying herself to sleep every night, because what kind of hideous life is that? For Alan, for either one of them? She'll have to get a second job to pay for his physical therapy and his drugs and his diapers, and she'll get run down and end up sick herself. She'll have to sell the house and rent a room in some flophouse with a single dirty mattress in the most godforsaken part of town, although the flophouse will have a nice name, like Paradise Gardens, because the nicer the name, the worse the flophouse, everybody knows that. Eventually she, Alan's mom, will develop consumption. She'll crawl into bed with drooling Alan at Paradise Gardens, and they'll pull up the covers and she'll tell him everything's going to be okay, except clearly it's not going to be okay. Clearly it's the most horrible thing in the world, and one night, probably a Tuesday night, she'll look over at Alan while he sleeps, and she'll think that maybe she should just smother him to death. She won't actually do it, but she'll think about it. At first she'll think it's for his own good and she'll just be helping her son end his grievous suffering, but then she'll realize that it would actually be for her. It will end *her* suffering if she just quietly snuffs the life out of her misbegotten vegetable son. And she'll have to live with that forever, in secret shame and horror on top of the everyday shame and horror of Alan's constant pooping and drooling and helplessness.

And all because Charlie used his one allotted wish, the one everybody dreams of, for this—to send Alan Mears and his consumptive mom to a flophouse to die.

There's your sweet and gentle. What would Xiomara think of *that*? He almost wants to tell her when he gets home, just to get it off his chest. But he knows he can't.

"Say it again," Charlie said, when his dad first told him the new girlfriend's name. And then: "Spell it." Xiomara could have been the ugliest girl who ever lived and he would have loved her because of her name. You couldn't have a name like that without some crazy exotic magic rubbing off on you, could you?

Except she wasn't ugly. She was dark and Spanish and beautiful. That she also had a tiny left arm the size of an infant's, connected to a pretty little hand with painted nails, only made her more beautiful.

"Don't stare at her baby arm," said Charlie's dad. "That's why she's got tits, Jesus." Which drew a one-eyed glare from Xiomara that made Charlie's dad grin.

"'S okay, *chiquito*," she said. She leaned down, all breasts and one tiny arm, and stared at him hard. Evaluating him. And then, very slowly, she made a V sign with the first two fingers on her right, regular-sized hand, and held them horizontally across her right eye.

Charlie did the same, but with the first two fingers on his left hand, holding them horizontally across his left eye.

Xiomara nodded. "So, *mijo*, we understand each other," she said gravely.

And Charlie beamed.

"Weirdos," said Charlie's dad. Xiomara stood up and unleashed a gorgeous Spanish fury at him, and Charlie's dad laughed, and then the rest of the evening was a blur of El Salvadoran food and loud music, with Xiomara now and then flashing Charlie another sign from *The Thunder, Perfect Mind*, the sci-fi adventure show that Charlie and (as it turned out) Xiomara's nephew back in El Salvador both held dear. Not the horizontal V sign, no—that was only used, as Xiomara understood, for moments of intense and immediate spiritual recognition.

When she left, Charlie stood at the door and waved goodbye as his dad squeezed Xiomara's butt and kissed her.

After that, he saw Xiomara once a week, and then twice a week, and then pretty much every day. Mostly with his dad, but sometimes, more often as time went on, it would just be Charlie and Xiomara. They'd play *Tripa Chuca* or Crazy Eights and watch the latest episode of *The Thunder, Perfect Mind*, or they'd sit together on Xiomara's couch and find an old movie (she loved anything old, but especially, to Charlie's endless fascination, old Abbott and Costello movies). Or she'd ask him to talk to her while she got ready for her shift at Lucky's, so he'd read aloud from some poem he'd learned in class by Edgar Allan Poe or W. B. Yeats or Alfred, Lord Tennyson (he always stressed the comma). She said she just liked hearing him talk. His English, *muy exótico*. That anything Charlie said could ever be exotic was absurd, and maybe he knew even then that she was only being kind. He decided he was totally fine with that.

The months passed. One day his father called when Charlie was at Xiomara's and said he had good news and bad news. He asked which one Charlie wanted first.

"Bad?" said Charlie.

"Let's do the good news. Your mom called from Newport and got a boob job and we're getting back together."

"She was in Newport?" Charlie asked.

"Bad news is that we need some I guess you'd call it one-on-one time? Or maybe one-on-two time, ha ha? Seriously, though. Long story short, we're heading out of town. But we think an awful lot of you."

"Sure," said Charlie.

"See how it wouldn't have worked if I started with the bad news?"

Charlie agreed.

"'Mara there?"

Xiomara at that moment was in her Lucky's uniform, tiny shorts with four-leaf clovers covering each nipple. She grabbed the phone and listened, shouted in Spanish, said *Yeah, yeah, yeah*, rolled her eyes—she was a world-class eye roller—and flexed the fingers of her baby hand as she paced back and forth across the kitchen.

Charlie retreated to the other room, half listening, and opened Xiomara's laptop to research orphanages. Which he recognized as being not totally logical, but better an orphanage than a foster home. In an orphanage at least he'd be surrounded by rapscallions. They'd have great names like the Artful Dodger and Lefty and Snaggletooth and Bobby No Legs. That incorrigible scoundrel, Bobby No Legs. Who had a crusty exterior, sure, but a heart of gold. Always listening to Charlie's ideas, yelling at Lefty and Snaggletooth to pipe down because Charlie's onto something here, and then saying, "Go on, kid." Always calling

Charlie "kid" even though they were pretty much the same age, in fact wasn't Charlie actually one week older *exactly*, but still, hard to get upset with Bobby No Legs. Not because of his missing legs—a mystery, sure, and someday they'd find those crazy legs—but because of his tragic past, e.g., the suspicious fire at the Old Mill, right around the time that Old Man Muldoon was trying to buy up all the land, only he'd run into, let's just say, "resistance" from Bobby's parents, Dashiell and Mariposa. No. Roberto and Esmé. Although Esmé always went by "Cookie" on account of that time with her aunt—

"What's this?" from Xiomara, looking over his shoulder.

He started to explain. "You see, Esmé had this thing where—"

Xiomara sighed and closed the laptop. "Going to work, *mijo*," she said. "Pillows and blankets in the closet. I'll take you to school tomorrow."

In the morning Charlie went to school. Later, Xiomara picked him up on her way home from her housecleaning job and brought him back to her place. They had dinner. After dinner she washed dishes while he did homework, and then they sat curled up together on the couch and watched *Abbott and Costello Meet Captain Kidd*. Now and then she brushed his hair with her baby arm. When the movie was over, she put on her Lucky's uniform and told him not to stay up late. Charlie thought he should really get to work registering with his top-choice orphanages, and probably with at least a few safety orphanages, assuming you could register online for an orphanage. But for now, maybe, couldn't he just lay here on the couch? Just for a little while. Lay here and not be worried about anything, surrounded by Xiomara's things, the iguanas and movie posters and replicas of the Eight Wonders of the World and crystals and mirrors of all shapes and sizes, found treasures that were only treasures, maybe, to Xiomara. But they felt, oddly, like home.

The next day came and went, pretty much the same way.

And the day after that.

So he stayed with Xiomara. She never asked him to leave. One night after Sunday Sundaes she passed him a letter across the table. An official notice of adoption, signed by Xiomara and Charlie's dad and a judge.

"I know," she said, "it sucks, *mijo*."

Charlie stared at the letter. And then down at the table. Trying to find the word for this. This feeling right now, there had to be a word.

"I'll find it," he said, over and over, but Xiomara didn't understand because he was blubbering so much. Like a total nutjob. Xiomara said *Ah, Pooh Bear*, and brushed his hair with her baby arm.

She just loves him. So he isn't about to tell her about Alan Mears and his mom. Or about Steve-O and Big John and all the others. Because who wants an adopted son like that—hate-filled and friendless? Nobody does. If it takes throwing Steve-O off the water tower to keep things going, then that's how it'll have to be.

A sedan pulls up at a traffic light beside Charlie and he hears the rear window come down.

"Hey," a voice calls out. "Hey, Shit Bear."

Charlie doesn't look up.

"Hey," the voice calls out, louder, and Charlie recognizes Miggs, his nickname benefactor.

I wish, Charlie thinks.

"Leave him alone," says Trish Mackey. He knows it's her without looking up, knows the precise frequency of her voice, could probably— if it were an assignment, say, not something he'd do just for fun, of course—chart its specific resonances and spectral peaks on a graph. He tries to appear preternaturally focused on the task at hand, which seems to be staring down at his feet while trying to furiously blink himself out of existence.

"Fatty," says Miggs.

"Shut up," says Trish Mackey.

"Kidding around," says Miggs. "Hey, Shit Bear. Who am I?"

Against his better judgment, Charlie looks over. Miggs has pulled his arm down into his shirt so that only his hand sticks out. He wiggles his fingers and laughs as the light changes and the car speeds away.

Charlie stops and watches the sedan for a block or two. When it reaches Madison, it turns right. Then it explodes.

A mushroom cloud expands above Madison Street and windows are shattered for blocks in all directions. The force of the blast is so powerful that it leaves a ten-foot-diameter crater in the middle of the street. Miggs is obliterated. Just blown into like a million soggy pieces. But Trish Mackey escapes, miraculously unhurt. She brushes dirt and gravel and pieces of Miggs off her clothes and pulls her hair out of her face and looks through the smoke, flashing her glassy but still beautiful azure eyes in Charlie's direction.

The thing about a wish is that you only get one.

If you get even that, Charlie thinks, as he resumes his careful progress along the curb. Which, probably, you don't. But at *most*, you get one. Not three, where you end up using your last wish to take back your other, stupid wishes before they destroy you. So you've got to be careful, mindful of the classic pitfalls—asking for money, fame, beauty, success, talent, popularity. Forget it. Sooner or later it'll be your undoing, and something horrifying will come knocking on your door to send you screaming all the way to hell.

But you can think small.

You can wish for something innocuous that won't throw the universe out of balance and upset the gods. You could, for example, wish to be braver. You could wish to be kinder. A little more good-natured. How could that be bad? You could wish to be thin. Or not thin, but maybe just less fat. Nothing all that noticeable, except maybe to Xiomara, who already tells him once a week that she thinks he's losing weight.

You could make a wish for someone else. That couldn't backfire, could it?

A beat-up Volkswagen lumbers past him and into Adelio's parking lot a couple blocks away. Once or twice a week Charlie rides his bike to Adelio's from Xiomara's place—their place—and buys a candy bar. If he has extra money he'll pick up a magazine or some silly plastic ring or colorful hair ribbon for Xiomara. Maybe he'll stop in today and find some little treasure.

One wish.

He's struck by this strange thought.

What if, having made and been granted your one wish, you must forget that it was ever made at all? Like, for example, if you were lying on someone's couch at the end of a long day, and you wished that each day would start and end like the one that just happened. That life would give you nothing more amazing than that, day after day, and you'd be okay with everything else.

Crazy, Charlie whispers to himself. But the hair on his arms stands up, and he stops moving for a little while to think about it.

Meanwhile, Wade parks his Volkswagen in front of Adelio's and goes through the checklist in his head. He has the primary stocking and the backup stocking in case the primary stocking rips in half when he pulls it over his face. He has the money bag, aka Polly's lavender pillowcase with the white flowers. He has the gun. Does he have bullets? Check. And he has the handwritten robbery script on the back of one of Mel's inspirational note cards.

He's driven an hour and a half to get here and picked the store at random, so no one could possibly recognize him. What can go wrong?

Okay, let's start with *everything*. Everything can go wrong. It's a fucking crime. It's armed robbery.

He flips over the note card and sees Mel's calligraphy. *Visualize happiness now*. With the fancy blue and gold border. She can't keep them in stock, she says. An order for five hundred just this week!

Five hundred. Jesus. But God, it made her so happy.

Focus. Visualize.

Let's just say that he walks up to the register and says, "Give me everything in the safe, now, or we all die." Because this establishes that he, Wade, although nobody knows it's Wade due to either the primary stocking or the backup stocking, is willing to give up his own life for the sake of the job, which is what we'll call the robbery. Which implies that he's insane, yes, but doesn't it also imply a certain extraordinary level of dedication to the job? Which in turn suggests that he's a man of his word. It's not inconceivable that the appropriate response might be to just give Wade all the money and let him quietly go on his way. Maybe even feel a grudging admiration for Wade, this insane but dedicated and totally anonymous person who is willing to put his own life on the line and isn't just recklessly endangering everyone else like your run-of-the-mill criminal. Is it even technically necessary, just in like a purely moral sense, to call the cops afterward? Obviously Wade—that is, this anonymous primary- or backup-stocking-covered person here—has some compelling need for this money. Like, for example, Crazy Ed's Rent-to-Own Paradise. More specifically, monthly payments to Crazy Ed's Rent-to-Own Paradise that are approaching the four-figure range. The problem being that every time Wade goes in to make a payment—because Crazy Ed's only accepts in-person payments—he, Wade, has to walk past row after row of televisions, cookware, Tiffany-style lamps, faux-Persian rugs, electronics, jewelry, framed Rembrandt self-portraits, Parisian throw pillows, pashmina scarves, comforters, grandfather clocks, vacuum cleaners, and a million other things. But even that isn't the problem exactly.

The problem is Garbage Baby.

Eight weeks after Mel was born, she was stuffed in a garbage bag by her mother and thrown in a dumpster behind an adult video store. When she was found by the store supervisor the next morning on his way to work, she'd eaten her way out of the garbage bag and survived. Thereafter she was known as Garbage Baby. Everybody knew Garbage Baby, even Wade had heard of her from a couple towns over. Mel never complained about it. She never complained about anything, really. And she loved Wade, he could tell she loved him, but there was a part of her that just always seemed a little broken—like she was glad she'd eaten her way out of the garbage bag and was still alive and everything, but maybe it wasn't a great idea to expect a lot more than that from life. Maybe it wasn't a great idea to even want any more than that, even if other people she and Wade knew seemed to have a lot more. It wasn't disappointment, just resignation—the quietest resignation you could imagine—that Wade sometimes saw on Mel's face. So one Friday after work he stopped by Crazy Ed's Rent-to-Own Paradise and found a pair of sapphire earrings worth a thousand dollars, but he could get them today for just $9.99, plus another $9.99 per week for the next three hundred and eleven weeks. And in the morning when Mel came downstairs, she found a box wrapped with white and blue ribbons waiting for her on the dining room table. She looked happier than Wade had ever seen her, and when she undid the ribbons and saw the earrings, she cried and hugged Wade for a solid hour and told him that she loved him more than anyone had ever loved anyone, more than anyone could love or had ever imagined loving anyone else, and (sobbing wildly) that if she ever found out someone did love or could love or had ever imagined loving someone more, she'd find and kill that person. But it was the look on her face when she first saw the box waiting for her in the morning sunlight that Wade would remember forever.

When Mel went downstairs the next Saturday morning and kind of peeked into the dining room, just to see, she didn't say anything or even act the tiniest bit disappointed. But maybe there was a part of her that was, just the tiniest bit, disappointed. Maybe when she smiled at Wade it wasn't totally exactly the same smile she'd given him the week before. And so the next Saturday morning, there was a new gift (a stainless steel dual-cook convection toaster oven with ExactoHeat™ calibration sensors, the toaster oven of the future according to the sign at Crazy Ed's) waiting for Mel on the dining room table, wrapped in white and blue ribbons. Mel came down and peeked into the dining room and laughed like a girl on Christmas morning, and then hugged Wade and cried a bit. Except maybe she didn't cry as much, maybe she didn't tell him that if she ever found anyone on earth who loved or could love or had ever imagined loving someone more then she'd have to kill that person. So the next week there was another gift waiting for her, wrapped in white and blue ribbons. And the week after that. She was always happy to find the gifts, but now and then the smile she gave him was almost kind of sad, like she was saying it couldn't ever be like that first time. But Wade wanted it to be like that and refused to stop trying, so his tab at Crazy Ed's kept getting bigger and bigger. And one day soon—like this Monday, according to the letter he'd snatched from the mail pile before Mel discovered it—men will show up at the door and Mel and Polly will watch as the kitchen is gutted and most of the house and all of Mel's nice clothes and half of her jewelry gets hauled back to Crazy Ed's warehouse. Polly will run off to write a despairing blog post but her computer will be gone, so she'll reach for her tablet device but that will also be gone, so she'll write out her despairing blog entry by hand on a napkin and then scream when she understands that no one will ever be able to read it. Mel will say, "At least we've got my inspirational note card business to fall back on," and Wade will have to admit certain things concerning certain recent bulk orders. At which point all the light will go out of Mel's face, or at least the portion of the light that was ever in any way attributable to Wade. And he, Wade, will be the one who closes the door forever on this brief interlude of joy in Garbage Baby's life.

And that is the problem.

Focus. Sixty seconds and it's over.

Okay. What happens if—let's just say—he gets recognized as he gets out of the car? As he's pulling on the stocking? Maybe he looks over and sees Brad, the next-door neighbor. Kindly old Brad who sometimes shovels their sidewalk before they get home from work, and brings in their trash bin from the curb, and always waves and smiles at them, even the day he pulled the plug on Maura. Howdy, Wade. Polly's getting big, isn't she? Oh, things are fine with me, thanks for asking. Except that Maura's dead. Otherwise, though, things are fine. *That* Brad. Pulling in next to Wade's car, seeing him slide the primary or the backup stocking down over his face. Knowing the truth.

What then?

He'd have to kill him, wouldn't he? And then he's bound to get caught and sent to jail for murder. Would have to hang himself the first night in jail. Because why procrastinate? It's better to spend a few nights in jail getting raped? Or, Jesus, raping someone else. Because he'd have to rape someone to establish his dominance. Wonderful. Now he's a rapist and a murderer. So, definitely looking at a hanging in the very near future.

Unless.

Unless he's able to quickly stuff Brad's body in the trunk before anyone notices. Which sounds horrible, but what's the alternative? A life of rape and murder and jail time for a crime he didn't even commit? Sure he's committed murder if we're talking about Brad, and we probably should be, but in this scenario at least he hasn't robbed Adelio's. And nobody knows about Brad.

Yet.

But now he's got a body in his trunk. He'll have to, what, chop it to pieces. Or break all the bones so Brad will fit inside a sack or a suitcase or something. Is that horrifying? Yes, absolutely. But the thing is, that's the job. That's the discipline.

That's the discipline. What the fuck is that?

Better to just kill himself. New contingency plan: if you see anyone you know, shoot yourself immediately. Which seems weirdly rash. And yet the alternative is: Brad, folded into a suitcase, lying at the bottom of a river. Plus all the prison rapes, unless those are no longer necessary in this scenario, he can't remember. But either way there's Brad to consider. No matter what, Brad is dead.

He stares at the door to Adelio's. And he has this revelation.

Once when Polly was three or four, they all went to the beach. They had this thing they'd do where Wade would get down on his knees in the shallow water and turn his back to the sea, and whenever a wave was about to hit, Polly and Mel would shriek and point at the wave approaching behind him and he'd pretend he didn't understand what they were saying. He'd say, "Gorilla? You're saying there's a gorilla behind me?" And Polly would laugh and shake her head and shriek some more, and Wade would guess something else, like a blimp or Abraham Lincoln or a platypus. Finally he'd turn around to see the platypus and he'd get knocked on his ass by the wave. Polly would scream, and then when Wade popped his head up out of the water a few seconds later, looking like a drowned animal, she and Mel would laugh like loons. Then they'd start the whole thing over again.

The revelation that hits him, sitting in the Volkswagen, is that there's no way this ends without somebody getting hurt.

Ah, he thinks. Ah, Mel.

Ten seconds later he opens the door.

And everything, somehow, is perfect. The place is empty. Wade walks to the register and holds out the gun. He can barely hear his heartbeat and his hand is steady. Give me everything in the safe or everyone dies, he says. And the clerk, who is as old as Wade's dad, and looks like Wade's dad, just nods his head. He says, Okay, son, and holds up his hands. He says, Let me put up a sign so nobody else comes in while I open the safe, and Wade says, Good idea. Everything happening in slow motion, kind of. They go back to the safe and the old clerk stuffs the money into Polly's lavender pillowcase. The old clerk's hands are steady too. Like he's practiced this. He hands the pillowcase to Wade and holds up his hands, and says, Everything's okay, right?

And everything really is okay. Nobody gets hurt. Somehow this is all going to work out.

He hides the gun as he leaves the store. Gets in the Volkswagen and starts the engine, keeping his eye on the old clerk through the glass. No reason to panic now. He's home free. Of course that's always when something terrible happens and the plan falls apart, saying you're home free, and everyone in the audience just groans because it's such a stupid thing to say, or even to think, but he thinks it anyway. He backs up and turns the wheels so he'll be able to speed out of the lot, and in his rearview mirror he sees the kid, this fat dumbass kid, not paying attention to anything except his feet as he walks along the curb. Wade hits him so hard that the Volkswagen's rear bumper falls off.

He gets out and runs to the back of the car. Shit.

Shit.

Fucking fuck, kid.

Wade takes out his phone and calls 911. Realizes he's still wearing the stocking so he pulls it up off his face. He tells the operator there's a kid down on the sidewalk by Adelio's, that he's hurt bad, and then he hangs up and stares at the phone for a second. Turns it off.

Ah, fuck, kid.

He leans down. The kid's crying. Hard to tell how bad it is. Maybe he'll be okay, maybe he won't. But the kid's crying. He's trying to reach his phone, which was thrown aside by the impact. Wade retrieves it and puts it in the kid's hand, but the kid drops it immediately.

"Can't," the kid cries. "Please. Call her."

Sirens. In Wade's head, maybe?

"Listen," he says. "Somebody's coming, kid. Hang in there."

"Call her," the kid says again. "You have to."

"I can't stay," Wade says.

Definitely sirens.

"Please," the kid says. Crying. Scared.

Damn. Fucking damn, kid. Polly's age.

He takes the phone.

"Who," he says. But he doesn't have to ask. All the calls and all the texts are from the same number.

He calls, and when a woman picks up, he explains. Tries to explain. She cuts him off and tells him that's she coming, that she's on her way. Half-mad but coherent enough to tell Wade that he, motherfucking Wade, has one job, and that job is to stay there and make sure Charlie is okay. Nothing he will do in his entire life will ever be as important, she says, as this one thing. Nothing can happen to him. Nothing. Does he understand? Does he understand, *cabrón*, that nothing bad can happen to this kid? That the fate of the motherfucking universe depends on it? The rest is an eruption of Spanish profanity that Wade unfortunately and completely understands and will remember for the rest of his life.

I understand, he says, I get it.

Hold his motherfucking hand, she says, so he takes Charlie's hand. He sets the phone down and tells Charlie that she's on her way. The kid's still crying.

He can see the ambulance now, and the police cars.

He tosses the stocking to the ground. Thinks that he should probably call Mel. Explain, well, probably too much to explain. Maybe just tell her that he's fucked everything up pretty bad. That he's sorry, for whatever that's worth. Probably nothing.

Jesus, the kid's such a mess. Still crying but trying not to. Trying to be tough.

"Hold on," he says.

What the hell. It can't hurt to say it.

"Everything," he says, "will be okay."

Tom Howard's stories have appeared in *Ninth Letter, Indiana Review, Cincinnati Review, Willow Springs, Booth,* and elsewhere, and have been awarded the Robert and Adele Schiff Award, the Tobias Wolff Award, the Masters Review Short Story Award, and the Indiana Review Fiction Prize. He holds an MFA in Writing from Vermont College of Fine Arts, and lives with his wife in Arlington, Virginia.

CPSIA information can be obtained
at www.ICGtesting.com
Printed in the USA
BVHW081732110219
539977BV00019B/500/P